THE
FORGOTTEN
HEADLINE

THE
FORGOTTEN
HEADLINE

The Summersville Series
BOOK 1

MCCAID PAUL

Cover Illustration by © 2017 Damonza
Edited by Josh Vogt
Book formatting by SGR-P Formatting Services www.sgr-pub.com/services
ISBN-13: 9780999614525

DEDICATION

To Dad,

who inspired me to write

CONTENTS

PROLOGUE

THE KILLER, AS you should call him, was nervous. His adrenaline formed a tight knot in his stomach, making him feel queasy. His hands were shaking uncontrollably; beads of sweat broke out on his forehead, and he blinked rapidly. The gun was aimed at the back of the driver's head. He tried to hold a firm grip on the gun, ready to squeeze the trigger if anything went wrong.

"Drive faster," the killer barked at the driver, strands of spit flying from his mouth.

The driver, a man, pushed his size ten foot down on the accelerator, exclaiming, "Look at what's happened to my wife!"

The killer sat between two girls in the backseat, one of whom held a baby in her arms. He constantly looked out the back of the car. He had to make sure no one was after them, especially the police.

The young, trembling girl on the left of him was crying as she stared at the gun aimed at her dad's head.

The teenage girl on his right side shook with fear as she cradled the baby. She replayed the events back in her head: the man jumping in the car just as her dad was driving off, the bullets flying through the windows, spraying glass into everyone's lap; the killer ordering her dad to go at gunpoint. Two of the bullets had torn into her mom, sending a scream echoing through the car. She had watched as her mom's neck went limp and how her head fell lopsided across her shoulder. She was dead. The girl knew the police hadn't meant to do it; they were only trying to shoot the man who now held them as hostages.

The teenage girl squeezed the baby to her chest, snapping back into the present.

"Don't shoot him, please!" The teenage girl's plea sent the baby into a crying fit.

The killer turned, face contorted in rage. "Shut the

baby up, before I do!"

The young girl watched the strange man scream at her sister and became even more terrified. She tugged on the door handle, but it was locked. She wished she could escape; she didn't want to be shot.

Before anything else happened, the car came to a stop. The killer pointed the gun at the teenage girl. "Don't move or I'll shoot!"

The teenager looked away, not wanting to see the man's eyes. That was all she could see, the black ski mask covering everything but his eyes and lips.

She wondered what would happen. Would the man kill them? Would her dad save them? Her thoughts were frantic.

The killer threw the little girl from the car and onto the ground, aiming his gun down at her. She heard her sister plead before a gunshot shattered the air. The teenager screamed with such ferocity that her face turned as red as blood. She sprang from the car, leaving the baby on the seat, and launched herself onto the killer's back.

The driver opened the console and grabbed his own gun, the one he had in case of an emergency.

The teenage girl put up a fight, kneeing the man in the back, digging her teeth into his shoulder, and burying her fingernails into his neck.

The killer cried out, "Get off me!" He screamed and grunted several times before he shook her to the ground like a bug. He aimed his gun at her, ready to shoot.

A scream echoed off the trees louder than the gunshot itself as the killer fell onto his back, dropping his gun. The driver, still aiming the gun at the killer, ordered, "Stay down!"

Blood poured through the killer's fingers as he clutched his wounded shoulder. He got up, grabbing the gun and held his one free hand in the air.

The driver was helping his daughter up when it happened. The gunshot startled the teen, making her jump in alarm. She turned to face her dad only to see him on the ground, blood covering the leaves like a spilled drink.

The killer laughed, even through his excruciating

pain. The knot in his stomach was gone and now only adrenaline fueled his excitement. He saw the explosion from the end of the gun and then the girl drop like a bowling pin. He wore his smile proudly as he remembered that he had only one thing left to do.

He peered back into the car, searching for the baby. His smile faded into a frown. There was nothing but an empty seat where the baby was supposed to be. He circled the car to see if the baby fell onto the ground. After several minutes of intense searching, the baby was nowhere to be found. He threw the gun down and screamed. Several obscenities rolled off his tongue; hatred swelled up inside him like a balloon taking in helium.

The baby was gone. The only fragment left of this family. Where was the baby?

11 YEARS LATER

2014

1

THE HUNT

THE DAYS HAD turned cold. The warm months seemed to be just a memory now, the bitter coldness stinging Mick's skin every time he walked outside.

Slipping his boots on, Mick Smith sighed, knowing it would be another one of those cold days. But the fact that he was going with his dad to squirrel hunt was the only thing that made him happy. He grabbed his .410 shotgun, slipped on his camouflage jacket over his white t-shirt, and ran through the house to the front door where his dad was waiting. His dad's hair was ruffled in a mess, making it look like a squirrel had crawled around in it. His dad never combed his hair, always letting it look as though he should do something with it. It always made Mick angry, but he never said anything to his dad. His dad didn't care how he looked, he only cared how he acted. He had always told Mick that it doesn't matter about your appearance, all that matters is how good you are inside. And his saying went along with his appearance.

His dad smiled at him.

"Where are we going today?" Mick questioned.

"Over there by the gate in the woods." His dad pointed so Mick could see where he was talking about.

"Now remember our gun safety rules I been tellin' you about."

"Yes, dad." Mick remembered the long conversation his dad had explained to him: never point your gun at a person, unload your gun before climbing a fence, and never stick the barrel in the dirt.

Dad crossed a fence, stepping over it with his long stride, as he pushed down on the top wire. He moved ahead, looking back and said, "Work on getting over the fence. You can do it."

Mick propped up his gun to cross the fence safely.

He struggled to place his foot over the top wire. He pushed down on the top strand but his legs were extremely too short to step over it like his dad. He fell, unceremoniously onto the ground and scurried to get back on his feet. His dad moved ahead, failing to wait on Mick. Retrieving his gun, he moved quickly, trying to catch up with his dad, almost running through the bushes.

They moved through the large oak trees, stopping a few minutes to listen for noises and sounds. His dad instructed him to look up into the upper limbs to see any movement from squirrels scurrying to the safety of their nests. Mick obeyed and looked up.

"The branches will usually shake when a squirrel is running along them. If you see anything, aim as close as you can and shoot. Remember to keep your gun tight to your shoulder when you shoot so it doesn't kick and bruise you like last time."

Mick remembered last time when he fired and he had it against his arm and it gave him a big bruise. He was glad he had done it, so he could learn his lesson.

He leaned against a tree and heard the noises of the forest. A woodpecker hammered on a dead tree, making it sound like a distant drum. A high-pitched bark of a fox echoed through the woods and a large limb fell to the ground with a heavy plop, making Mick jump in fright. His heart beat rapidly, as his mind tried to sort the different sounds.

A mockingbird rested on a branch peering at the two figures below him.

Whispering to his dad he asked, "Can I shoot it?" He pointed at the bird.

"No. Wait for a squirrel, we can't eat a bird," his dad said as he stared up at the tops of the oak trees.

"We can feed it to the cat." Mick's eagerness melted when the bird flew away. In spite of his disappointment, he still waited. His hopes lifted when he heard the chattering of the squirrels. Mick couldn't help but smile. He held the gun to his shoulder, ready to fire.

All of a sudden, his dad pointed to a branch where a squirrel was scurrying across. Mick lifted the gun and aimed closing one eye. Mick, with great determination, fired. The squirrel jumped at the force and pain of the shot. It plummeted down to the ground, crunching the leaves beneath it.

Mick ran to the squirrel. The squirrel's eyes were wide open and it seemed to look straight through him. Mick smiled, knowing he had killed it. He picked it up and saw where he had shot the squirrel directly through the heart. His dad smiled at him and laughed.

"I knew you could do it."

This was Mick's first time squirrel hunting. He had only been deer hunting with his dad twice before. His dad set up a big wooden board in the back yard and he shot at it with his .410 shotgun for practice. His dad was serious about hunting. When Mick was four he had him in the yard shooting birds with his BB gun. Now here was Mick, holding the shotgun with one hand and the squirrel with the other looking as though he had just won a medal. Blood dripped from the gunshot wound onto the ground. His dad put the squirrel in a small game pouch and they moved on. Careful not to make too much noise, Mick stealthily stepped without dragging his feet.

One thing Mick favored the most was to be in the woods. Even if they went deer hunting and didn't see anything, or shot and missed, Mick always loved just being there, tromping through the woods and letting the cool breeze blow through his hair. He enjoyed the noises of the birds, the chattering of the squirrels and the other sounds that flooded his ears with what he called the joyous music of the woods.

Mick loved having a gun. He always wanted the one that would fit him the best. One might feel too long or too heavy. That's why when Mick got the right one he felt like he was unstoppable. He felt like he could shoot anything in the world and nothing could stop him. Mick was a country boy. Not one of those city boys who went around getting everything they wanted, whenever they wanted it. Not one of those boys who hated being in the woods, shooting at animals. If he could ever make a wish, it would be to live in the woods and to be alone.

"Dad, do squirrels always come out?" Mick asked,

barely over a whisper.

"No. If it is cold and windy, they will stay in their nest to keep warm. They will always see us before we see them and stay hidden for a while till they feel it is alright to come out of their nests."

"And when they come out and think they are safe from us, we fire, right?" Mick questioned with a puzzled look.

"Correct." His dad moved ahead. Sometimes Mick figured that his dad was ignoring him. He never wanted to get in the conversation with his son about girls, or anything to do except hunting (or homework). He liked reading but only westerns or books about the woods. He was just like Mick, he loved the woods.

As they passed a dead tree limb on the ground they heard a snap in front of them from the bushes. His dad put a hand out to signal him to stop.

Mick did.

They could see the deer's big ears sticking out of the bushes like giant antennas. The deer snorted and blew in alarm as his head rose, alerting to their scent. An explosion broke the tranquility and Mick realized his dad had fired his rifle. The deer must have jumped twenty feet in the air before disappearing back in the bushes. Smoke hung in the air from the rifle. The deer was gone. Mick started to protest, but his dad interrupted and said, "Be patient! Let's not chase him. He will bleed out in a few minutes and we'll find where he lays."

Mick smiled and asked, "So, did you hit him?"

"He won't go far." Mick knew that his dad was confident that he had shot the deer.

Mick started to move towards the direction of the deer. His dad grabbed his arm. "No. We wait for at least ten minutes to give him time." Mick got the hint.

Ten minutes passed by quickly and his dad pointed at the blood trail, following the deer's path. Mick noticed that they were crossing their property line and the neighbor's fence.

"Dad, we shouldn't be on the neighbor's property. That's trespassing!"

"We'll be fine. If we don't make too much noise,

we won't get caught." His dad looked ahead and then said, "Just stay quiet."

His dad didn't hesitate to stop at the property line. They had been warned many times by the neighbor not to go on his property, but Dad had to get his deer. He was responsible for getting meat on the table.

"Dad, this isn't right. You know the neighbor. He's very dangerous," Mick said, stopping and looking back.

The neighbor was a mean man with very cruel intentions. His name was Richard Welch, one of the most disliked people in Summersville. He was the kind of man to kill people or injure them for being on his property. Mick almost reached out to stop his dad but failed to do so. He was already way ahead of him.

Several questions went through Mick's mind, sending a chill down his spine. What if the neighbor was watching them? What if he was waiting out there in the woods to shoot whoever was brave enough to test him?

That is when the danger began, right there at that moment. A loud popping sound went off and Mick realized it was the sound of shots being fired at them. Bullets collided into trees, ripping through the bark. Some tore through the leaves at full force, others flying through the air, ready to enter their next victim.

Mick darted, keeping low to the ground as he ran, his dad following behind him. Bullets whizzed by Mick's ear, missing him by inches.

Mick stifled a scream, running as fast as he could off of the property. He didn't stop until he reached their front yard. His dad ran and knelt down in front of him.

"I'm sorry. I wasn't thinking. Are you all right?" His dad looked Mick all over to make sure he hadn't been hurt. "I ought to go over there and take care of him! It's one thing to shoot at a grown man, but to shoot at a boy…"

Struggling to breathe, Mick looked around in a daze. His head felt heavy, his heart pounded in his chest, and his body shook with fear. Bile crept up his throat and into his mouth. Mick spit the bitter acid on the ground, wiping his mouth with his sleeve.

"I'm fine," Mick lied, "but we need to get our deer

back without getting shot."

His dad stood back up and put a hand on his son's shoulder. "We will leave the deer; it is not worth getting killed over. I hope you realize that."

Mick nodded in agreement, but his thoughts said otherwise. The wheels were already turning in his head. He had to get that deer without getting shot. He would go back to search for it without his dad's knowledge.

2

MR. WELCH

MICK, FEELING ANXIOUS, said quietly, "Maybe we should call the police."

His dad looked at him with confusion. "Why? What are they going to do about it? You know the police just think he's crazy."

"He shot at us! He should be arrested!"

"It doesn't work like that, Mick!" His dad said, clearly frustrated with his son. His lips were pinched together and he was shaking his head. "It's not that simple!"

"I wish it was! He's dangerous! He's a homicide waiting to happen!" Mick yelled, clenching his fists.

"You're too young to understand!"

"No, I'm not!"

Mick wanted to explode with rage, but kept his cool.

"Yes you are! I want you to stay away from his property and away from him! Do I make myself clear?"

Mick stuttered, "Y-Yes, B-B-But…"

"Just go to your room!"

His dad ran a hand through his hair and let out a long sigh as he turned towards the kitchen.

Mick stood his ground, staring at the back of his dad's head. As he disappeared around the corner, Mick followed him.

"I'm going outside." Mick started to walk away before a hand clamped tight onto his shoulder.

"Stay away from Mr. Welch. Don't go anywhere near his property."

Mick gave his dad an icy stare that said a thousand words.

"Don't worry. I won't."

Mick's dad took his hand off his shoulder and looked away from his son. Mick was already out the door when his dad shouted, "I mean it, Mick!"

Mick kept a cold face as he went over the steps of the plan in his head.

1. He would run to Mr. Welch's property line.

2. Then, he would tiptoe across and wait for any gunshots.

3. If there were none, he would stay low and away from Mr. Welch's house. He would look for any signs of a blood trail.

4. When he found the deer, he would tie a piece of rope around the deer's neck and drag it back.

5. When he got home, he would tell his dad that he had found the deer dead a little ways in the woods. He would lie to his dad and tell him the deer had run back onto their property instead of going farther onto Mr. Welch's.

Mick went around to the shed and grabbed a long piece of rope. He imagined the rope to be a large snake. He laughed at the childish thought.

He was determined to get the deer no matter what happened. As long as his dad didn't find out about it, everything would be fine.

Mick closed the shed door and took off across the lawn to the woods. He tried to stay away from the line of sight through the window. His dad might be watching him, he might be anticipating Mick's every move. He shuddered at the thought.

Squirrels scurried and birds flew off their branches when Mick invaded their part of the woods. He ran through the woods until he came to the property line. He took a deep breath. As he let it out, he courageously tiptoed across. Mick waited for any sudden sound of gunfire. After several seconds, he started on his way. He stayed low, careful to not be seen.

Mick could make out the side of Mr. Welch's house from the woods. Smoke drifted into the sky from the chimney. The barn door was banging in the wind.

Mick saw no sign of the old man and smiled. He continued to search.

. . . .

Mr. Welch sat with a serious demeanor. His eyes were dark, his mouth twisted into a frown. His stare was unfocused and his breathing slow. Mr. Welch had been like this every day now.

Heavy silence blanketed the room. A dark cloud seemed to be hanging over Mr. Welch's head.

Mr. Welch was going through a serious wave of depression. His somber appearance almost made him look like a dead man.

Over the past few days, he had tried to commit suicide. He had stared at ropes and guns in a different way. It seemed like they were doing him a favor, seeming to say, "Just take me and pull the trigger and all your sadness and memories will wash away." But every time he almost did it, when he almost ended his life, he stopped himself. He told himself he needed to face life like a man. He needed to fight his inner demons.

He wondered what his father might think of him if he could see him now. Would he give his son remorse? Or would he think he had failed at being a father?

Mr. Welch had done some good things in his life. He had saved a few lives and sometimes even attended church. But if you heard all the bad things that he had done in his lifetime, you would forget about the good things. You would question them. They would drift from your mind like smoke.

Mr. Welch hated that the environment kept changing. It was hard to keep anything hidden since the ponds and rivers kept drying up. This year had been the worst with the heat that was for sure. Mr. Welch was thankful for the cool wind and the bitter cold.

The heavy blanket of silence was uncovered as Mr. Welch jumped up. He heard the barn door banging in the howling wind outside. He cursed to himself for leaving it open. He had almost given himself away. If someone had gone inside, he might have just killed himself for sure.

Mr. Welch snatched up his gun and pulled on his coat. He yanked the front door open and a powerful gust of wind almost threw him back. He stepped onto the porch and closed the door. The continuous bangs of the barn's door and the howling of the wind tapped out a rhythm. The repetitive noises made Mr. Welch want to go insane.

After quickly locking the barn door, Mr. Welch started to walk back to the porch. Before he could though, movement from the woods caught his eye. He turned his head and raised his gun. A small figure was creeping very quietly through the woods, staying close to the ground.

Mr. Welch cursed. He ran towards the figure, pointing the gun in front of him.

"Whoever you are, you're getting it this time. Not letting you come back over here again!"

Mr. Welch had to fire his gun at someone in the woods this morning too. He had almost started to shoot one of them, but decided he didn't need his list of offenses to include murder. He didn't want to be defined as a cold-blooded killer.

A sudden thought came to Mr. Welch, almost making him stop dead in his tracks. What if the figure was the girl? What if it was *her*?

Mr. Welch laughed at how stupid the thought was. *No, it couldn't be.*

He ran ahead, confident that he would get whoever

this was once and for all.

. . . .

Just as Mick thought he was going to get away unnoticed, a yell from back at the house shattered his hopes. Mick had been spotted. He looked behind him and froze. The old man was running in his direction, his gun aimed at the boy.

Before Mick could even move, Mr. Welch fired at him.

The sound of gunfire sent the boy darting in the other direction.

Mr. Welch caught a glimpse of the figure before it ducked down behind several bushes. He couldn't let him get away.

"I know you're here! You can't hide from me!"

Mick could feel his heart beating a hundred miles an hour through his chest. "Don't catch me. Please, don't catch me," Mick whispered, now taking long, deep breaths. Mick could hear him coming closer. He held his breath, trying to make as little noise as possible.

The footsteps ended.

Mick waited for any indication that he had turned around and went back home.

Mr. Welch aimed his gun at the bushes and fired.

Mick jumped up as the bullet zipped by his neck. He took off, running farther into the woods.

Mr. Welch fired shot after shot at the figure. The figure ran wildly, running here and then ducking low and running in a different direction. It appeared he was trying hard not to stay in one place so he would be harder to shoot. Mr. Welch had to stop him, he was heading towards his beaver pond.

Mick's adrenaline sent him into turbo speed. He ran faster than he ever remembered. He didn't have time to think, he just ran. He went in one direction and then another, proving to be an impossible target.

Mr. Welch continued to shoot until the gun gave a loud click. Mr. Welch yelled, throwing it down in the leaves. He sprang forward and ran. Compared to Mick's pace though, Mr. Welch was only doing a slow jog. He tripped and his face made impact with the ground. Pain shot through his head and blood poured out his nose.

He pulled himself up and spit out a wad of leaves that had gotten in his mouth from the fall.

Mr. Welch cursed and rubbed his pounding head. Shaking a fist, he screamed, "STOP!"

He screamed after the figure until his voice suddenly became hoarse.

. . . .

After the bullets stopped, Mick continued to run until he felt the threat had passed. He plopped down at the base of a tree and gathered his breath. He told himself to calm down and breathe. He trembled in fear and gripped the piece of rope tightly, scared that Mr. Welch would continue to follow him until he was sure Mick was dead. He tried to shake the thoughts away, but it was like trying to get cat hair off a sweater, nearly impossible.

Mick should have listened to his dad. He should have taken his idea under advisement. He should have realized how dumb he was to think he would get away without being shot at. What if he had been killed?

Mick knew that Mr. Welch was someone he needed

to avoid. The old man despised people with a keen loathing. Many people thought he was too crazy to even live around.

Even the police hated going to his house, preferring to go in groups of at least four officers. Like Mick said, he was a homicide waiting to happen. Someone was going to eventually get shot.

Mick looked in front of him.

He gasped.

Straight ahead lay an old beaver pond. Most of the water appeared to have been dried out by the heat. Mick's mouth fell open in surprise when he saw the deer lying in the pond, its blood staining the water a dark red. The deer's eyes looked ahead as if it had seen something before it bled out.

Mick's eyes darted in the direction the deer was looking. A bunch of bushes were piled high from the water's surface, almost as if they were covering something.

Mick slowly walked towards it. He took a step into the cold water, which felt like ice against his skin. Mick tried not to think about it, instead devoting his attention to the mound of bushes and limbs ahead of him. In just a few more feet he reached it, the water only coming up to his ankles.

He moved one of the branches and shattered pieces of glass fell away into the water. Mick moved more of the branches, throwing them down behind him. He could see part of a broken windshield and the hood of a car. He set to work, throwing off limbs and branches as fast as he could. His fear was replaced with excitement at his discovery.

Eventually, a red car was visible that appeared to have been beat up and wrecked. The hood of the car was crumpled, and the headlights were broken as if they had hit a tree, or something solid. A long crack ran the length of the windshield. Mick couldn't seem to understand what was holding it together.

The entire vehicle had been underwater at some point, causing rusty spots and a thin crusty ring circling the car. The ring looked like a chocolate milk stain on a glass.

He went around to the rear of the vehicle. To his dismay, the license plate was missing. This added even more to the mystery of the car. It seemed that this was another fact that proved that whoever this car belonged to, they wanted it to remain hidden. He noted the brand of the car, a Ford Mustang. It was red and large enough to seat five people.

Mick noticed something that made him question what he was seeing. Several round holes in the front right door of the Mustang made Mick's mind race in question. *Were these bullet holes? Was someone doing target practice on the car? Where did this car come from? Why was it left in this old beaver pond? Should he investigate the mystery a little bit more before he told his dad? Should he go get the police instead?*

Mick ran his fingers over the bullet holes on the car door. The holes were smooth in some places and rough in others depending on whether they went in or came out of the car. Mick put his finger through one of the holes, trying to convince himself that they were real. He took his hand away from the car door. He rubbed the smashed hood of the car with the same hand he had rubbed the bullet holes with, almost cutting himself in several jagged places.

Mick knew he would have enough trouble getting the deer back to his house, and he decided not to tell his dad about the car. Besides, his dad might get suspicious. What if he found out that the car was on Mr. Welch's property? Then he would know where his son had been. Mick couldn't let that happen. He would investigate on his own.

Mick proposed a theory: over the course of time, the beaver pond had been filled with water and sometime in the past few years the water had come down, revealing the car.

Mick tied the piece of rope around the deer's neck and began to drag the animal. He stopped a few times to catch his breath. When he got to the property line, he took a big sigh of relief, thankful that he hadn't been killed or at least shot.

. . . .

Mr. Welch limped towards his house. He had to

hobble on his left foot; he must have twisted his other one from the fall. He wondered if he was delirious and maybe had just seen what appeared to have been an animal or something not real. He could just imagine how silly it would look for someone to see him shooting at something that wasn't even there. Mr. Welch questioned his own sanity. His idea that the figure had been an animal quickly faded as he wondered if it was really human.

Mr. Welch, afraid that his eyes had been playing tricks on him, could have sworn the figure had been a child.

3

THE DEER

MICK'S DAD WAS happy and angry at the same time. When Mick got the deer in the backyard, he yelled for his dad to hurry to see what he had retrieved. His dad ran around the house, staring at what Mick had brought. His mouth fell open and he shook his head. Mick could almost feel the lecture coming. To his surprise, his dad reached out and hugged him.

"Mick Smith! What did I tell you about going on that man's property?" It was obvious he had mixed feelings.

"I told you not to go back over there! But I am glad you got the deer and that you're safe."

Mick hugged his dad, feeling proud of himself, but

deep down inside, he felt scared for his life. *What happened to the people in the car? Were they killed?* He shivered with fear. He hoped his dad wouldn't question him anymore. Mick knew that if his dad continued to, he would crack.

Mick tried to tell his dad that he had found the dead deer on their property, but his dad didn't fall for it. He was smart at figuring things out. Mick hoped his dad wasn't smart in figuring out that he had almost been caught by Mr. Welch and had made a shocking discovery on his neighbor's property.

Questions about his neighbor piled up inside his head. *Was Mr. Welch involved in the mystery of that car? Was he the one that made those bullet holes? Does Mr. Welch know about the car? Was he the one that covered the car up with those bushes and tree limbs so no one could find it?* Mick wondered if the thoughts were true about the old man. The car *was* on his property. He had to have something to do with it, right? Mick shook the thoughts away.

He tried to think about something else. He looked

46

towards his dad, who was now examining his work.

Mick's eyes ventured to where his dad had hung the deer by its head. His dad never hung it by its hind legs, so it wouldn't be too messy. Other deer hunters cleaned their deer by hanging it by the back feet. Mick's dad had been taught by his father to do it the other way.

"Go get me one of your golf balls," his dad said. Mick came back within a minute and gave one to him. He watched his dad place the golf ball in the hide of the deer's neck near the slit that his dad used to bleed the blood from the animal. Taking a short piece of rope, he tied it around the hide and the golf ball. His dad, using all of his weight, pulled down on the rope. Mick watched the hide peel off of the deer inches at a time. Within a few minutes, the deer hide was in a pile beneath the buck.

His dad took a gut-hook blade on a special skinning knife and pierced the purplish skin of the deer just beneath the throat. He slid it very slowly, opening the cavity that held the lungs, heart, stomach, and intestines. The organs, or guts, as his dad called them, spilled out, leaving the intestines hanging on a small piece of tubing at the anus. Mick smelled a vile odor that consisted of gas from the guts and blood. In spite of the nauseous smell, Mick was surprised that he didn't get sick to his stomach.

With a water hose, he washed the deer out and finished cutting little places that they didn't need to keep. The hooves, head, and hide were discarded, leaving a pinkish-purple carcass of the buck. It went into an oversized ice chest and they filled it with ice and water.

With the deer finished, dad turned his attention to Mick. "I'm proud of you and I'm also mad. That old man is crazy and will shoot you! I'm just so glad you're safe." His dad hugged Mick again.

Mick turned to leave. His dad watched the boy as he walked away, a smile widening across his face. One of those smiles that said he was hiding something.

. . . .

The house sat in silence.

Mick trudged towards his room like a zombie, a

hundred different thoughts running through his head. He thought about Mr. Welch, and how the old man had almost killed him. How would Mick pull it off next time? He thought about his discovery, wondering if Mr. Welch even knew that the car was on his property. Maybe the old man didn't. Maybe Mick was the only one who did. He thought about his dad, who didn't believe Mick's story. Of course his dad didn't fall for it. He could always seem to tell when Mick was lying.

Mick's mind was consumed by all of these thoughts. They never seemed to end.

They might not have ever if something in the hallway hadn't of caught his eye. Mick stopped abruptly, turning around to face what he had passed.

The old wooden shelf was lined with pictures of him and his dad. Some of them were taken at places such as the bowling alley or the swimming pool, others on holidays like Thanksgiving.

Most of the photos were taken by his mother. He still saw her goofy expression when she'd snap the picture, trying to get Mick to smile. It almost made him laugh just thinking about it.

The younger Mick smiled back at him from the shelf, revealing several missing teeth. He appeared happier than he was now; it was true life had taken a huge toll on him through the years.

Mick scanned the photos, looking for one of his mother, but he knew better. She was absent from every one of them, almost as if she never existed.

Almost as if she was never there at all.

4

BILLIE

MICK WENT TO one of his only friends, Billie Hagan. She was a country girl who loved bossing people around, but she was a good friend to Mick. She was a straight-out tomboy and always had been. Mick knew she always would be, unless a miracle occurred. She was sassier than a cat any day of the week and could have a temper as fiery as a dragon's breath. She had straight blonde hair that fell over her shoulders and piercing blue eyes that could cut into you. She was in the same grade as Mick, the fifth.

He traveled down Billie's long driveway, stirring up dirt and running over rocks and sticks that snapped underneath his wheels, barely missing a toad frog at the last second.

It was usually a five minute bicycle ride to Billie's house, but he could get there leisurely in about ten.

Soon, the house came into view. The large, white, two--story structure rose high above the ground, making Mick feel small. He swore he saw a figure at the picture window, staring out at him through the glass.

The inside of Billie's house didn't fail to impress. It was nice, if not better, than what the outside of the house was like.

The first floor consisted of a den, dining room, and kitchen. The most impressive part of Billie's house was the spiral staircase, which led up to the second floor landing. Billie spent most of her time up there, mainly in her bedroom, where she sat at her desk on the computer or watching TV. Along with Billie's, there were also two more bedrooms and a large bathroom.

Mick was slightly envious of Billie's house. He was happy for her, but at the same time wished he had something similar. He always enjoyed his visits to Billie's house, silently comparing hers to his own. His was also two stories, but was a lot smaller than his friend's.

On this particular day, Mick needed some advice. He needed to know how to find that certain car and what year it was made. He sat his bicycle in their yard and knocked on the front door. Within a few seconds, Billie opened the door and said, "Well, howdy. What are you doing here?"

"I need to know how to find the make and model of a particular car and what year it was made."

"Well, don't you sound rehearsed? All you gotta do is go to the internet and look at pictures of that vehicle till you find a type that looks like the car you are looking for. It should tell you what year it was made and everything you need to know when you click on it. Why come to me with a question like that? Couldn't you ask your daddy?"

Mick sighed. "I didn't want to tell anybody this, but...I discovered something in Mr. Welch's old beaver pond. You know, my neighbor, Mr. Welch."

Billie sighed, rolling her eyes. "Get to the point."

"Well, a deer that my dad shot went on the old man's

property and when we went to go find it and take it home, the old man started firing shots at us! Later, I found our dead deer at an old pond on his property. In the pond, I found a car that had bullet holes in it. I think the old man has something to do with it."

"What did you do with that deer?"

"Billie, don't you get the point? That old man probably killed somebody in that car and crashed it in the pond to hide the evidence."

Billie's eyes widened. "Wow! This is serious."

"I know. That is why I need the answers to find the exact car model and what year it was made. If I can get that information, I can check the media at that time to figure out if anything happened to that car. If a killing was committed and the same car model went missing, I would have evidence that the car was on Mr. Welch's property. There were bullet holes in it, Billie! This evidence would make the police think it was Mr. Welch that was behind the case. This mystery could be solved!"

"Did you look at the license plate number?"

Mick shook his head. "To me it adds even more to

the fact that whoever is behind this wants the car hidden."

Billie just stared at him, dumbfounded.

"So, you think that old man has something to do with it?"

"Of course I do! I just have one more question for you."

Billie crossed her arms and cocked her head like a sassy, city girl. "Well?"

Mick questioned, "Can you possibly help me with the case?"

Billie, revealing a small gap in her front teeth, smiled.

"I'm in." They high-fived each other.

"Ask your dad if you could come to my house to help me find the information about the car."

"I will. He'll say yes…hopefully." Billie started to run out the door then turned around with a greedy smile.

"What do you want now?" Mick asked, rolling his eyes.

"Could you bring me some deer meat?"

"Oh, just go find your dad!"

While Mick waited, he thought about the case. Billie came out a few minutes later and gave him good news. She could come over and help him.

....

Billie wanted to help Mick out for one reason and one reason only: to possibly see if this case was connected to her mother's. No one had ever figured out what had happened to her. She had gone missing when Billie was only seven. Billie was convinced that her mother was murdered. She knew that her mom wouldn't just run off and leave them; she had loved them too much. Ever since she was young, Billie wanted justice for her mom. That would be a dream come true if she figured out anything. But if she didn't, wouldn't this be a waste of time?

Billie's thoughts wandered away from her mother and to a reward. *What if there is a large reward for the car? If I collect the reward, what could I buy with my share? I always wanted a four-wheeler and a new saddle.*

Billie smiled to herself. This case might turn out to

be fun after all! But she was wrong. If Billie knew what danger this case involved, she might have stopped Mick or told him he could do it himself. Neither of them knew what they were getting themselves into.

5
THE OLD MODEL

BILLIE AND MICK leaned in close to the computer, their shoulders rubbing against each other. Earlier, Mick had ran up the steps to his room and blushed when Billie had reminded him of how messy it was.

"How do you live like this?" Billie asked, picking up items from across the room and throwing them onto Mick's bed. Billie had been in Mick's room before, but it had been a while. She used to come over and play with him, but they were getting older and they didn't go to each other's house for playdates anymore.

Mick sat in the chair at his desk in front of the computer. Billie sat next to him, watching Mick log in. It had never occurred to her that she would be trying to solve a case with her best friend. But here she was with Mick, trying to solve a case that could have bigger consequences than they could even imagine.

Mick typed in 'Red Ford Mustang' and a bunch of models popped up. Then Mick saw a picture of one Ford Mustang that matched the one that he had seen at the old beaver pond on Mr. Welch's property. He clicked on it, and saw that the Mustang was a 2001 model. Mick smiled.

"Looks like we found our car model," Billie said, staring at the screen.

"So, now all I have to do is find old newspaper headlines or stories about a missing car. I could also check for a missing person in town who may have been murdered along with the car. That would explain the bullet holes. The car had to have disappeared at some point and the family reported it missing." Mick paused for a moment, putting a finger to his chin. Billie glared at him impatiently.

To an adult observing them, it might look silly, but they had a high diet of mystery novels, and since the opportunity had been laid before them, they were committed to solving this mystery.

After several seconds of lingering silence, Mick asked, "How would I find old newspaper headlines, Billie?"

"At the library. They have newspaper headlines from way back."

"You always know everything," Mick said with a laugh.

"Well, ain't I supposed to? I'm a girl, you know."

Mick ignored Billie's comment. "Then we have to go to the library. A newspaper story about a missing car might help us solve the case. We will know when the car disappeared. We can tell the police that we found it in Mr. Welch's old beaver pond. The only thing that won't be answered is why Mr. Welch was hiding a car in the first place. Why doesn't he want it to be found?" Just as Mick got the words out of his mouth, Billie gasped. She grabbed Mick's arm and beamed.

"Mick! That's why he was firing shots at you and your dad! He doesn't want anybody on his property and doesn't want anybody finding the car in his beaver pond!"

"Billie, you are a genius!" Mick exclaimed. Before Mick could stop what was happening, he wrapped his arms around her, sending a scream from Billie.

"What in the world are you doing!?" Billie yelled as tiny drops of spit flew onto Mick's face. She pushed him away.

"Sorry." That was all he could manage to say.

. . . .

When Billie left, Mick fell back onto his bed. They had a new lead in the case and Mick was astounded. Suddenly, Mick realized he was sad. Even though the case was on his mind, another thing was, too. His mother always returned to his thoughts when he was sad, depressed, or upset. These were the moments when he was the weakest and he couldn't block her out of his mind like he normally did. He preferred to forget about her and that painful time in the past. But here he was, his mother working her way into his brain almost as if she was trying to tell him something. He closed his eyes, on the brink of a dream, and let the memories of her flood through his mind. He dreamed again of the day she came in the door, tears streaming down her face, leaving a long line of mascara. She had run to him and picked him up like he was as light as a feather, squeezing him until he couldn't breathe.

"Mick," she had said, "I love you so much. I won't let anything ever happen to you!"

Mick had felt remorse for her; maybe she had had a long day at work or maybe had gotten into a fight with his dad. Whatever it was, he liked the way she held him close; the way she had told him how much he meant to her; the way her words were like a soothing lullaby.

He wished she were still here. He often tried to find a picture of her, a way to remember her by. But it was like she never existed, like she had only been the product of his imagination.

It was times like this that he just needed someone to hold him close. He needed someone to be there and hold his hand. His dad would never be like his mom. His hugs were never quite the ones his mom gave; his words never quite as soothing. A single tear slid down his face and he felt his throat tightening.

"Mom!" His words escaped like a desperate cry for help. "Where are you?"

Tears rolled down his cheeks like a crying baby.

He didn't get to say goodbye, and the only thing he remembered was her talking to him that morning before school. He wished he could have at least talked to her one more time. He wished he could have said just one more "I love you" and given just one more hug.

His thoughts went back to the day she died. It happened when he was in school. He remembered the strange man coming to the school and taking him to Billie's house and Billie's mom hugging him, still not knowing what had happened. He remembered his questions, the answers he got and then the despicable and horrifying truth: his mom was dead. He remembered how he shook his head and yelled, screaming, "NO! She can't be! She wouldn't leave me!"

His mind always went back to her in his darkest hours; in those times that were the most difficult.

As the tears rolled down his cheeks, as his throat tightened like it would close up, and as his cries continued for his mother, his thoughts evaporated and sleep consumed him.

6

THE FORGOTTEN HEADLINE

THE NEXT DAY, they found themselves walking up the steps of the public library. Little did they know, in just a few hours, a startling truth would be discovered.

Mick walked up to the librarian and put his hands on her desk. She looked at them from over her computer.

"How may I help you today, young man?" She asked Mick with a serious face.

"We would like to know where the old newspapers are."

The librarian began to smile. Billie realized how small and petite she looked, making her wonder if she was anything above ninety pounds. The librarian got up and the two kids followed. She came to a desk in the far corner of the library where hundreds of newspapers were stacked.

"They're stacked by their year."

Mick started rummaging through them without saying anything to the librarian. The librarian stared, expecting a nice "thank you," but Billie and Mick had no time to tell the old, tiny woman thanks. They had to find a headline that would help them with the case. The old woman muttered something under her breath and walked away, back to her computer at the main entrance.

Since the car was a 2001 model, Mick rushed through the 2001 newspapers. He skimmed the pages looking for anything about a missing person or a red Ford Mustang. After he was finished with one of the newspapers, he would hurriedly throw it down and begin on the next one.

Billie looked through the 2002 newspapers just in case the person or the car had gone missing around then. She did it more methodically than Mick, actually folding them back up when she was done.

After thirty minutes, she became bored and plopped back in her chair. She closed her eyes, feeling a headache coming on. She heard Mick going through the papers and throwing them down in frustration. Billie opened her eyes and sighed. She looked down at the newspapers and at the large stack that she had left. Her eyes glanced over to the other newspaper sections where she saw the same large stacks. Not knowing why, a sudden impulse came over her to look through another stack.

Billie got up and walked towards one stack where a newspaper lay on top, left open. Snatching it from the stack, she folded it into its correct position. She started to put it back but a large headline on the front page caught her eye. She read it slowly, placing her finger underneath every word of the headline. Her mouth fell agape in surprise. She started to turn around and show it to Mick, but stopped herself. She didn't want to disturb him, he was preoccupied and would ignore her anyway. Besides, she didn't need to show it to him; it wasn't any of his business.

Billie ran back to her chair, holding the newspaper tightly in her hands. She placed the newspaper on the chair, leaning down to grab her backpack off the floor. She unzipped the top of the backpack and grabbed the newspaper. She quickly looked around to see if anyone was watching her. When she didn't see anyone, she stuffed the newspaper in her backpack and zipped it back up.

Billie looked over at Mick, hoping he hadn't seen her. He hadn't, he was still going through the newspapers like a determined detective. She exhaled loudly, revealing a small smile as she sashayed back over to the 2002 newspapers like nothing had ever happened.

After two hours of intense searching, Mick was exhausted.

"I give up," Billie said flopping down into a chair. Mick sat down next to her.

Maybe we will never find it, Mick thought.

Billie sighed. "Solving a case is harder than it appears."

Mick looked at her and with a hopeless tone, said, "I

didn't say it would be easy."

Mick looked at the newspapers that laid scattered out on the desk. He stared at them for a minute until he saw something that caught his eye. One of the newspapers in a different stack which was labeled the year 2003, had a small headline with a big picture underneath it. Mick jumped up and stared at the headline. When he read it, his mind almost went blank. It read:

THE JOHNSON FAMILY VANISHES

Red Ford Disappears after Gunfire by Police

Police gave chase to a bank robber that escaped in a red Ford automobile. The robber was unidentified. He wore a black ski mask. Police say that the Johnson family had just gotten into their car when the robber hijacked the family at gunpoint. The police fired multiple rounds at the robber. The car sped off and was not seen again. After hours of searching, the police found no evidence of the car or family. "They just vanished and we can't seem to find any of them.

We couldn't find a speck of evidence of where the car, the family, or the robber went," Police Chief Mike Rodriguez said in an interview a week after the incident.

The fire department employees found an infant identified as Mick Johnson at the main entrance of the fire department. After investigating the incident, police have identified the infant as one of the missing family members of the kidnapped family. Police will try and determine how the baby ended up at the fire department. The rest of the family's fate is still unknown. There is a ten-thousand dollar reward for information on the family's whereabouts. The FBI has been contacted due to the bank robbery and the possible kidnapping of the family. This story was submitted by Benjamin Dover of the Summersville Daily News.

Mick wanted to scream. *Mick Johnson? Was that him?*

Mick looked at the photograph underneath the

article. It showed a teenage girl standing next to the man who he assumed was their father and a little girl standing next to the woman who he assumed was their mother. In the woman's arms was a baby, whom he was assuming was him. In the background, it showed the red Ford Mustang.

He didn't know of any other 'Micks' in Summersville, and he did remember the one time his dad accidentally slipped up and sad, "Mick Johnson! Get back here right now!" He had just assumed that his dad had misspoke, but now he wasn't so sure if that was the real reason.

No, Mick thought. *My name's Mick Smith.* But how could he be so sure? Had his dad been lying to him? Mick never had that many pictures of when he was an infant, but he never thought anything of it. Now, it seemed that he should have.

Billie got up and looked at what her friend was staring at. She gasped. Mick stared at the paper, dumbstruck.

If this was him, his whole life was a lie. His dad, who

always took him hunting, was not his dad. His mother that had died when he was six was not his real mom. He remembered when he used to ask his mom about when he was little and when he was a baby. She could never tell him much and now he knew why. His *real* mom was the one that knew everything. She had been the one that held him and rocked him. Even though his mom that died when he was six held him and told him how much he meant to her, now he knew she wasn't his real mom.

Tears fell like raindrops from his eyes, the hot tears rolling down his cheeks. Billie was still reading the article when the librarian came over to see what was wrong. The old woman tried to get Mick to talk, but he was ignoring her. He was thinking about the case, the case that led to the truth about his own life. And yet, what made it worse was that his dad had never tried to talk to Mick about the disappearance of his family. He probably wasn't Mick's *real* father. And another thing, Mick was born in 2003, putting another idea in his mind that the baby was possibly him.

He just cried, until he couldn't anymore. He

wondered what other things he didn't know about his own life. How many secrets had his parents been keeping from him? Were they always lying to him? Did they think that would make things better?

The Johnson Family Vanishes. The headline. He kept repeating the sentence in his head until he thought he would explode with question. Was it a forgotten headline? Or was it well known in this town?

If it was forgotten, he had a lot to worry about.

The librarian patted Mick's back with her little hand and said, "It's okay, honey. Tell me, what's wrong?"

Mick wiped the tears out of his eyes. He turned to face the oblivious librarian who looked down at him like he was a little kid. The look in her eyes told him what she was thinking.

"I'm fine. I just found a newspaper article that was sad, that's all."

The librarian whimpered and poked out her lips. "I'm so sorry, dear. If you need anything, I'll be right here."

By the way she said it, you could tell she thought

Mick was a little sensitive.

As she started to walk away, Mick shouted, "Wait! I have a question."

The librarian stopped and turned to face Mick, a small smile widening across her face. "I'll have an answer."

Mick took a deep breath and replied, "This headline says 'The Johnson Family Vanishes.' I read the article and it says that a family went missing along with their Ford Mustang. The police tried to find a robber that hopped in the family's car. The car drove off along with the family. No one ever heard from them again. Except for the little baby, Mick Johnson, who was found on the fire department steps?"

"Oh, yes," the librarian smiled, "I remember that." She had a faraway look in her eye as she gazed out the window behind Mick. "Sadly, though, the case went cold and everyone seemed to forget about it."

Billie looked from the librarian to Mick, and asked, "Then the case was forgotten?"

"Yes, of course. No one wanted to think about such a

tragedy. They didn't want to think about a family possibly being murdered." She continued to look out the window as if she were transfixed. "Nothing like that had ever happened in Summersville, until then."

"Then this means," Billie paused, "that it's time to solve the case once and for all."

The librarian looked confused. "I agree! The case does need to be solved, but not by kids. Are you trying to solve it yourselves?"

Billie looked at Mick and smiled. Mick looked at the librarian and said, "Yes. If the police won't solve it, we will."

"Don't you know what danger you're walking into?"

The sudden question hit Mick right in the gut. The reality of what they were doing made Mick think. *How could he answer her question? Did he really know what he was getting into? Were his and Billie's lives in danger?*

"Yes, we're fully aware of the situation," Mick said, knowing it was a lie. He looked towards Billie for some comfort, but all she did was stare.

"Dear me!" The old woman gasped, trying to sound

sincere. She put a hand to her heart, her mouth open wide.

Mick and Billie didn't fall for her act.

"You sure are brave. I never could have done such a thing at your age."

"What you have to realize is this mystery revolves around my childhood. *My* life. At least," Mick said, a confused expression on his face, "I think it does. I have got to figure this mystery out, even if it kills me."

The librarian looked as confused as a fish in a dishwasher.

The way she scrunched up her face, a small question mark formed between her eyebrows. He didn't understand what she was confused about. Did she think it was confusing that kids were solving this case? And not the police?

"Well, I'm sure you won't get very far with this. You are just children. Children are supposed to be in school, not solving some *case*," the librarian spat with a sickened expression, as if the word had left a bad taste in her mouth. "They just don't have the time."

Billie balled up her fists and started to come towards the librarian. Mick held out his hand, motioning for her to stop. She paused, looked at the librarian like she was the one that had murdered her mother, and stepped back.

"Well, have a good day. We hope we solve this case," Billie grabbed Mick's hand and finished by saying, "without your help."

They were halfway through the library when the librarian said, "Wait! You haven't put the papers back in their piles."

Billie turned to face her and shouted, "Oh, I'm so sorry, *dear*! I thought children were supposed to be in school. Like you said, we just don't have the time."

Billie yanked on Mick's arm and they ran out of the library. Mick just hoped when they had solved the case, the librarian would know that they had.

7

THOUGHTS AND MEMORIES

THE NIGHTMARE HAD come true. His parents weren't really his parents. The dad he had grown up with and come to know wasn't the one that kept him as a baby, wasn't the one that held him and looked down in his eyes when he was an infant.

When you are a baby you have so many funny memories, but dad, of course, didn't know Mick's funny memories. His dad had come to know him, but his real dad was the one who he should be with. Where was his dad? Had Mr. Welch been the man who robbed the bank and hopped into the car? What had Mr. Welch possibly done to his dad? The thoughts were too much to bear. What if Mr. Welch killed his dad? Why hadn't his "dad" told him about this yet? Did he possibly think that Mick would learn this himself? Mick let the thoughts roll through his brain, making him furious and confused.

Complete thoughts.

Who put him on the steps of the fire department and why there? Why not a family's house? How hadn't the police found any evidence as to where his family was and the other things like the car and the robber? Did Mr. Welch kill his family? Why did Mr. Welch crash the car in the old beaver pond if he was the one who did?

Thoughts.

And the question that made him hurt deep down inside like never before. Like someone you loved died and you wouldn't see them again. Ever again. The question made him wonder what happened to his parents and made his heart leap into his throat. That question could only be: Did Mr. Welch kill his parents in cold blood and crash the car in the pond to hide evidence?

And Mick could only hope it wasn't true.

Thoughts.

Thoughts that wouldn't leave his mind until he solved the case.

Thoughts.

Thoughts that would lead him to his past. Complete *painful* thoughts.

. . . .

"Mick, are you okay?" Billie asked, after they had left the library and started on their way home.

Mick, his thoughts interrupted, muttered, "Yeah. I'm fine."

"You know it might not be you. Maybe your name isn't Mick Johnson. You never know."

"I know it's me, Billie. It explains why I don't have pictures when I was a baby and it explains why my dad misspoke that day and…"

Mick stopped his bicycle. He couldn't seem to take it all in.

Billie slowed her bicycle and stopped. She looked back at Mick with worry written all over her face.

"I shouldn't have told you to come here. I didn't

know that we would find something like this!"

Mick stared at the ground, letting the past flood him with memories. He heard Billie's voice but refused to listen.

Like a movie reel, the memories from first to last seemed to line up in Mick's mind waiting their turn to show him their view of the past.

First, came the memory of Mick's mom and dad sitting down with him at the dinner table, helping him blow out the candles on his birthday cake.

Next, came the memory of Mick's mom and dad hugging and saying that they loved each other.

Then came the memory that made him question his last: if they loved each other then why did they fight and scream? Mick still remembered their first fight and how he had locked himself in his room. He still remembered that night when he had held his hands over his ears as tears streamed down his face. He wanted to block the yelling and screaming out of his ears; he wanted to hide until the fight stopped. He replayed the memory over and over again at times when he was the maddest with his dad. It gave Mick an excuse to blame his dad for something. When his dad got mad at Mick one time for throwing a tantrum when he didn't get his way, asking him to repent to God, Mick had said, "Why do you ask me to repent? You never repented when you hit Mom and gave her that ugly bruise! Mom told me you never even said sorry!"

Mick remembered when the fight reached its climax and he heard the scream that made his blood run cold. His dad had shouted, "Don't raise your voice at me!" Followed by that came nasty language that Mick wouldn't dare repeat. He remembered when he had screamed out, 'Don't hurt her! Don't hurt her!' over and over again until he had lost his voice.

The next morning, he woke up to find his mom examining a bruise on her cheek with a mirror.

"Where's Dad?" Mick questioned, fear evident in his voice.

He would always remember that look she gave him, that look that made him wish he had never asked that question. That look seemed to ask him: "Why would you ask about your dad after what he did to me?"

"He left last night. I don't know when he's coming back."

Many nights just like that continued for the next few months until his mom's death. It always terrified Mick when those fights broke out; it always made him wish it was only a nightmare, not real life. He always wished one day to find out what happened to his mom, but his wishes always failed to materialize.

Then came the memory of his mom frantically telling him that it wasn't safe there anymore. That his dad was too violent and never wanted her to be in control. She grabbed Mick's arm and said, "I asked him about his childhood and I asked him about his life before we got married, but he said he doesn't like to discuss the past. I think we should go, Mick; it feels like the only option."

Mick always despised his dad when he was little, never wanting to speak to him whenever he laid his hands on his mom. He had always loved his dad before the fights, but not so much after.

The next memory was of the day after the strange man picked him up from school and had taken him to Billie's house. The day after Billie's mom finally confessed and told him that his mom was dead. It was the day that Mick's dad came to get him and he had to say his goodbye's to the Hagans.

His dad had looked tired, with dark, purple bags bulging out beneath his eyes. Mick wondered if his dad had gotten any sleep the night before. Billie's mom had told him that his dad would be with the police and might not return until the next day. Maybe they had questioned him all night long.

"Bye," Billie had said as they started to drive off. Mick waved, but his dad shared no signs of returning the nice gesture.

In the car, there was silence. Mick had so many questions piled up inside of him that he was afraid he was about to bust. Mick, breaking the silence, asked, "Why did Mommy leave us? Is she with God?"

"I don't know, Mick."

Mick started rattling off more questions, each time

getting no more than an 'I don't know' or 'stop asking me'. His dad's jaw tightened every time Mick asked a question and his brows furrowed.

Then, Mick noticing how angry his dad looked, cried, "I'm sorry! Please don't hit me like you did Mommy! I don't want any bruises!"

"Mick, I'm not going to hit you for heaven's sake! Stop bugging me with all your questions and accusations! Can't you see what I'm going through?"

A tear slid down Mick's face and his lip started to quiver. Mick looked away, not wanting his dad to see him like that. Not wanting his dad to see that he was crying.

When they got home, his dad went to his room and shut the door.

Mick stayed outside. But a question formed in his mind and wouldn't seem to go away. After an hour, he couldn't bear it any longer. He ran into his dad's room only to find him lying on his side, clutching the sheets and crying uncontrollably. He had grabbed his dad's arm and waited until the crying stopped. It never did.

Billie put a hand on her friend's shoulder and whispered, "Mick?"

He didn't move.

She lifted her hand to slap him, but decided that would only make things worse.

Mick didn't pay any attention to his friend, he was still in a daydream.

"Dad, how did Mommy die?"

The crying turned into sobs and he started to shake. Mick waited until his dad spoke, "Go away, Mick."

Mick trudged away and when he got to the bedroom door, he looked back and saw his dad as he had never seen him before. He saw a man that was unrecognizable, a sobbing shell of the former man he used to be. To Mick, he looked like a young child who had been torn apart by the madness of the world; like a tortured soul deprived of everything he loved.

A tidal wave of sadness had seemed to hit Mick then, causing the young boy to release his dungeon of emotions. He leaped onto his dad's bed and hugged him tightly, burying his face in his back. The young boy let out a wail, squeezing his dad tighter than he ever had before. His dad clutched his son's small hand, putting it to his reddened face as he let out his pain. Mick cried along with his dad, hardly caring about the damp sheet that clung to his bare chest. He didn't care about anything at that moment, only wanting his mom back. Only wanting someone to tell him how this had happened to her. Only wishing for her to be there, holding him and singing into his ear. Only wanting his questions to be answered and his sadness to be gone.

For years after his mom's death, his mind always went back to that day. The day he had seen his dad an emotional wreck. The day when he wished that his mom was still there with him. The day that Mick started to wonder if his dad had murdered his mom.

8

FACING DAD

MICK STROLLED INTO the yard, throwing his bicycle on the grass. He walked into the house, his dad right behind him. Mick wanted to blurt out his thoughts and confront his dad, but instead went into the kitchen to get a glass of water.

A noise behind his back confirmed that his dad had followed him closely. A hand gripped his shoulder and a voice spoke, "It's time you tell me about some of these problems you're dealing with."

"What do you mean?" asked Mick.

"Don't like you talking to that girl, Billie! Used to, but not anymore."

Mick's heart raced, wondering how much his dad

knew about his trips to the library and researching the old car. Mick turned and faced him. His dad looked strangely serious and stared into his eyes. Mick looked away, the first one to blink.

Mick finally spoke, "Billie is my friend and she understands things…"

"You will stop hanging around her. I forbid that girl being on our property and I'll flog you short of your life if I catch you with her." Mick's dad had a violent tone and it scared him.

"Dad…I need to…" Mick was almost crying in defiance.

"Don't start that with me. I'm not your mommy and she isn't here to baby you. It's time for you to start acting like a man and I'll see to it."

"Who am I?" Mick blurted out. Mick's dad grinned a cruel smirk and jabbed his son's chest, hissing in a mean voice.

"Raise your voice? So, you going to be a man now? Good, I like that…when I bust you in the mouth for that attitude…you can take it like a man."

Mick tried to back away, but was corralled and trapped by the kitchen sink. His dad pushed him harder and pinned him, putting his hot breath in his small face. "Last I checked, you are my boy, that's who you are."

Mick was trembling and afraid, hoping he wouldn't end up with an ugly bruise just like his mom had.

"You had something to ask?" Mick's dad asked, as if it were a contest for male dominance.

Courage from somewhere filled Mick's brain. Maybe it was the thoughts, maybe it was the idea that his dad couldn't hurt him bad…not kill him…just a spanking… an awful beating maybe….maybe a punch in the mouth. The words blurted out in frustration and contempt, "Where's my birth certificate? Did you adopt me?" A tear or two trickled down Mick's cheek.

"Where did that come from? That girl, Billie? Who have you been listening to?"

"N-No one," Mick stammered, looking away from his dad's menacing glare.

"LOOK AT ME!" Two strong hands gripped his shoulders and he was flung onto the kitchen floor. The man stood over Mick and prodded him violently with one of his feet, kicking him in the stomach.

Mick tried to yell out, but every time he did, a hard kick in his side would stop him.

His dad took him by the arm, snatching him up. He sat him down in a kitchen chair. Mick couldn't breathe and words would not come from his mouth.

Mick's dad took a chair and sat opposite Mick, slapping his face in an attempt to get Mick's attention. "Look at me, boy! Where are these questions coming from?"

Catching his breath, Mick finally looked at the man he had formerly called Dad. Mick thought about this man and how he changed so suddenly, so quickly. Was it the questions or was it that Mick had confronted him? How much of it was drama for the effect or was it a genuine mean spirit?

His dad slowly gathered his demeanor and now returned to normal. He looked at the floor and seemed to act apologetic. "Look...I probably acted a little crazy...let's start over. Ask your question. What do you want to know?"

It took Mick a moment to answer. Was it a trick? Was his dad going to hit him again if he asked the question?

"Am I adopted?"

"Where did you get that idea from?" Mick's dad didn't deny it and avoided the answer.

Mick was still afraid and hesitated to ask it again. He looked up at his dad, looking for a sign of what was going to happen next.

"Did that girl Billie tell you?" asked Mick's dad.

"No, I saw a picture at the library!"

"What kind of picture?"

"A baby was left at the fire department after a family went missing," replied Mick.

"And why are you so suspicious?"

"Because that baby was me."

Complete silence. It seemed like it lasted for minutes.

"How do you know it was you, Mick?" His dad questioned, breaking the silence and staring intensely at his son.

"It said my name in the newspaper article." Mick gulped. "Well, not my actual name. My biological name, I'm guessing." Mick looked down in his lap, avoiding to meet his dad's cold stare. "I couldn't help but read the story when the headline caught my eye."

His dad's eyes widened. Mick realized the words took him by surprise. He didn't dare confront his dad about the time he had accidentally called him Mick Johnson. He might just hit him again.

"Let's talk about this later," his dad mumbled.

Mick got up from the chair and slowly walked to the stairs. His dad had never hit him before; had never kicked him or screamed in his face. What if his dad had killed him? What was his dad hiding? His mom said he didn't like to discuss the past. Mick thought, and then he knew. Something in his mind told him that his dad might not have only killed his mom, but may have killed his family too.

Mick gripped the railing. He thought back to when they had been a happy family; to when his dad had really loved him and his mom. Mick cursed at his own dumbness, realizing for all those years before the fights and his mother's death that his dad was not who he appeared to be. His dad could only be described as a monster.

9

THE PHONE CALL

MICK STOPPED ABRUPTLY when the phone gave a loud, shrill ring. He heard his dad grumble under his breath and pick up the receiver.

Then there was silence. Complete silence.

"Hello?" his dad shouted into the phone, annoyed.

He answered a second later, speaking softly. "Oh, Mr. Welch."

Mick took a few steps down the stairs to hear more clearly.

"I think the boy is onto us." His dad's words took Mick by surprise. Did his dad know about the car? He took several more steps. This conversation was getting interesting.

His dad's voice fell to a whisper. "I think he knows that I'm not his father. I think he knows he was adopted."

Mick wanted to scream. Was his dad working with Mr. Welch? Was his dad involved with the missing car? Why was his adoption between him and Mr. Welch?

His dad knew the truth. His dad adopted him and never told him that he wasn't his real dad. His dad could know that Mr. Welch killed the family and they were keeping it a secret. And why did his dad adopt him? Wouldn't he want to kill Mick if he was the one that helped Mr. Welch kill his family?

Mick couldn't seem to stop the thoughts and questions.

"We have to do something about this, Richard!" his dad hissed, calling Mr. Welch by his first name. His quiet tone dispersed and was now very loud.

"Mick and Billie are getting close to the truth! They might blab everything to the police and we could end up in jail!"

There was another pause. Mick put his foot on the

last step at the bottom of the stairs, gripping the railing so hard that his knuckles had turned white.

"We can't let this happen!"

Mick couldn't take it any longer. He leaped off the bottom step, bursting into the kitchen. "I will figure out what you are hiding! You're not getting away with this!"

His dad slammed the phone down and howled, "You're not even sure what you heard! Don't jump to conclusions!"

Mick ran out the front door, his dad yelling after him. He ignored his dad's pleas, picked up his bicycle, and took off.

Mick hadn't managed to close the front door, leaving it wide open. He pedaled hard for several seconds before he looked back towards the door. His dad's body filled the frame of the doorway. All Mick saw when he looked back was his dad's menacing scowl and his dark eyes that were filled with hatred. His dad's appearance reminded Mick of a cold-blooded killer.

Looking ahead of him, pedaling as fast as his legs could go, Mick hastened, continuing to accelerate forward. His heart felt like it was beating out of his chest. He didn't even think to breathe or blink; he just raced on, determined to reach his destination.

He had to talk to Billie. They were in danger. His dad knew everything. Both him and Mr. Welch. He headed to Billie's house as thoughts poured through his head.

Was his dad going to kill him and Billie for knowing the truth? Was he really involved in the killings? What if he wasn't? What if this was just a prank?

No, Mick thought. *It can't be a prank. More like a bad dream, maybe.*

Mick tried to fight back the tears, but they just burst out of his eyes, flooding down his cheeks.

His parents, his name, his whole life: it was all a lie.

Mick couldn't stop. Not now. Not ever. He had to find Billie before it was too late.

10

DOUBT

Billie slinked upstairs like a housecat, quietly closing her bedroom door. Tears welled up in her eyes and she knew the floodgate was about to open. She swallowed hard and half-coughed, half-cried as she fought back her emotions. She grabbed the newspaper article out of her backpack, unfolded it and read it for the thirteenth time. The small black print, although harder to read than a normal print, was plain and to the point. The large headline though, said it all:

Well-Respected Nurse Missing, Presumed Dead
Summersville Police Department Criticized
Local Hospital Nurse, Candice Hagen, has been

missing for almost two weeks according to a Summersville Police Report filed four days ago. Family members are lost and police have no clues as to her whereabouts. Her car and purse were found abandoned at the Spring's bridge in Henry County. Police speculate she could be a victim of suicide but no body has been recovered. A local fishermen gave a report of a suspicious person jumping from the bridge on Tuesday, October 12th early in the morning. Candice Hagen went missing on Tuesday, October 12th, the same day the fishermen gave a report to police. Candice Hagen failed to report to her shift that morning, alerting the family that she may be in trouble. Police did not interview the fishermen until two days after her car was found abandoned while Summersville police were canvassing the area. She is a registered nurse in the Nursing and Rehab Center of White Springs. She is also a 1995 Graduate of Henry County High School and got her nursing degree from the University of

Central Florida. Candice Hagen was well-respected and loved in the town of Summersville. Her husband of ten years, John Franklin Hagen, is not considered a suspect in her disappearance. She also leaves behind a seven year old daughter, Billie. Although the Summersville Police Department was criticized for not starting the search for Candice Hagen earlier, many counties in Florida use a two-day rule before they investigate missing persons. This story was submitted by Jennifer Neal of the Henry County Examiner.

Billie wiped her eyes on the back of her shirt sleeve, the tears leaving a small wet stain. She set the newspaper article down on the bed as she moved to the window. She put a hand against the wall for support. Her sadness and pain seemed to weigh down on her, making her feel as if she were about to fall. She stared out the window that overlooked the front yard. She tried to imagine where her mother's car would be if she were still with them. Her dad's white truck stood alone on the gravel a hundred feet from the front door.

Billie couldn't seem to believe the allegation that her mom had jumped to her death. Why would her mom kill herself? That question had pained Billie for a long time. She was convinced her mom was pushed from the bridge by an attacker. Billie wanted to believe that because she didn't want to face the fact that her mother would just leave her without saying goodbye.

Billie loved her mother deeply. She remembered them going to Sunday School at church and them eating breakfast together every day before school. Her mom had always tucked her into bed every night at 8:30. This was followed by a very short song that her mom would always sing to her before she turned the light out. Billie could remember this happening hundreds of times.

On rare occasions when her dad was not home, her mom would let her sleep with her. Billie remembered how safe she felt with her mom next to her. She could still imagine the scent of her mother's perfume and the fragrance of her hair.

Billie could never understand why her mother never

told her goodbye. She couldn't imagine her mom just leaving her and her dad; she loved them too much.

As soon as she thought about this again, the emotions would swell up in her throat.

Her dad had been a different person after her mother disappeared. Billie noticed that her dad could not look her in the eye. If he did, she thought she could see small tears forming in the corners of his big brown eyes. Maybe it was guilt or maybe it was the unknown. Either way, it had torn her dad's heart out.

To make it worse, her dad wanted to hug her more now. But when he did, she could feel he was on the verge of tears. Instead, he would resort to telling her stories of how he met Candice at college. They had been in love from the first moment they had laid eyes on one other. He truly wanted her to know that it was "love at first sight."

Billie had asked her dad, "Why do I make you cry?"

He had answered her with a soft and sad response. "You remind me too much of your mother. You are a clone of her, Billie."

John Hagen is a sales representative for a medical supply company. He wanted to be a doctor in college, but his career path led him into sales while Candice finished a nursing degree. He saw her often at the hospital where she worked and they continued to eat lunch and date outside of work. Within a year, they were married.

Billie knew they loved each other and that her dad could not have harmed her mom. This added to the confusion as to why Candice would have left him by killing herself.

Her dad had told her that her mom's car had been found at Spring's bridge where police speculated she took her own life. Neither of them wanted to believe that. She had no reason to.

Uncle David had brought a different perspective to this theory, further confusing Billie. Her uncle, a rough country man who was half drunk most of the time, kept her family in chaos with his problems. He was Candice's brother, which made him Billie's uncle.

With an automatic disdain for Uncle David, John

Hagen had very few kind words for him and discouraged Billie from listening to his ill-advised theories, especially about the disappearance of his sister.

Billie vividly remembered one day when Uncle David was extremely drunk and had let several sentences slip, making her question everything that had been told to her about her mother's case.

His exact words to her were: "Have you ever thought that your daddy might have pushed your momma off the bridge? He's not the man you think he is. Be careful."

Her uncle's words had scared Billie, even frightened her. She had never thought that someone inside the family may have wanted to hurt her mother. She may not have ever come to that conclusion if Uncle David hadn't mentioned it.

Billie slowly turned away from the window. She stared at her computer and the journal beside it. Suddenly, she got an idea. Forgetting her sadness and pain, she ran over to her desk where the computer and journal were. She had to write down her uncle's exact words, the words that made her question everything. Maybe his words would help her propose a theory as to what happened to her mother. Billie sloppily and hurriedly wrote—in tiny writing—her uncle's words on a page in the journal. Then, opening Microsoft Word on her computer, she began to type.

11

THE MISSING FORD MUSTANG

WHEN MICK GOT to Billie's house, he bolted up the steps, throwing his bike in the grass in their front yard. He flung the door open and ran up the stairs toward her room.

"Mick! Is that you?" he heard Billie's dad ask. He ignored him, racing up the stairs.

When he got to her room he saw her sitting in a chair next to the computer.

She sat intently, staring at the screen.

"Billie, we need to talk!" he shouted, out of breath.

Billie screamed, falling out of the chair and onto the floor.

"Don't scare me like that ever again, Mick!" She got

back in the chair.

"My dad was talking with Mr. Welch!" Mick told her everything after that.

"So you think that Mr. Welch and your dad are behind the killings?" Mick, wanting to cry, stared at Billie, wishing he could be in a normal situation like her.

"Yes." It was sad to think that his guardian was a murderer, but the evidence was definitely pointing that way.

"We need to go back to Mr. Welch's old beaver pond and see if the car is still there so we can have proof for the police. We have to turn Mr. Welch and my dad in before we end up dead ourselves."

Billie gulped. Mick continued to gather his breath, staring at the computer.

"What are you typing?" Mick questioned, raising his eyebrows.

"What? Oh," Billie said, grabbing the mouse and minimizing the screen. "Nothing."

"You were typing something."

"It's none of your business," Billie snapped, standing

up and blocking the computer screen with her body.

Mick looked down at the journal sitting on the desk beside her computer, where tiny handwriting littered the page. It was Billie's, and it looked like it was written in a rush.

Mick stepped forward and peered down at the writing. "What's this?" Mick asked, putting his hand on the page.

"It's none of your business!" Billie sniped, closing the journal on Mick's hand.

"OWW!"

"Oh…sorry," Billie muttered.

Mick rubbed it, glaring at Billie.

"I'm sorry! You shouldn't have been looking at it anyway!" Billie yelled in a sassy tone, grabbing the journal and tossing it on her bed.

Mick's glare fell to her backpack, which was resting on the floor beside her desk. Poking out of the backpack was what appeared to Mick to be a newspaper. His mouth fell open and he reached out to grab it, asking, "You stole this from the library?"

"No!" Billie screamed, snatching it from his hands and hiding it behind her back. "That's mine!"

Mick had hardly glanced at it before she had snatched it from his hands, but he had managed to read the headline.

"Your mom," Mick mumbled, then shouted, "It's about your mom!"

"Yes, nosy," Billie spat, "It's about my mom! And it belongs to me!"

Mick couldn't believe her; she was the last person he would have thought of to steal anything.

She looked away from Mick to the picture of her mother sitting on her bedside. He knew what she was thinking.

"My mother was murdered, Mick."

Billie flopped down on the edge of her bed, her bed springs squeaking.

"You don't know that. No one ever found her body." Mick reached out to put a hand on Billie's shoulder but she brushed it away.

"And I thought this case would have at least given

me some idea as to what happened to my mother. I thought I would at least have found something out."

"That can be our next case. We can find out who killed your mother. But for now, I have got to solve this one. My whole life is a lie."

"And what if mine is, too? You're so selfish, Mick! Don't you realize what I'm going through?" Billie started to cry and put her head in her hands.

"Billie, I'm…"

"All this time you've been thinking about yourself! You don't care about what happened to my mother, all you care about is what happened to your family!"

Mick thought about yelling at her but decided that would only make things worse. He realized that she was right; he had been too caught up in himself to even notice her feelings and mood that changed from time to time. He should have questioned why she was sad. He should have questioned how she felt about also not having a mom. Mick felt slightly ashamed of himself.

He looked over at the picture on Billie's dresser. It showed a woman in a field of dandelions, smiling like she didn't have a care in the world. Her clean, long blonde hair hung over her shoulders and her eyes were a piercing blue. He realized how much Billie resembled her. That day that he had stayed with them, the day that he learned of his mom's death, he never expected that Billie's mom would end up missing.

"I'm sorry, I didn't mean—"

"Let's go," Mick muttered, as he headed out her bedroom door.

Billie made up an excuse to her father that they were heading to the library so they weren't raising suspicion.

"We might be gone for some time." Her father bought it.

The two hopped on their bikes and headed to Mr. Welch's property.

They were silent the whole way.

At that moment Mick was sorry he had ever brought Billie into this. He knew it was hurting her to know that they were in danger and she might end up like her mother. But it was too late now. The wind blew against their faces and whispered in their ears; there was the chattering of squirrels and the sound of the bikes rolling along on the pavement. It all made Mick relax. It was peaceful out here in the country.

He almost stopped and told Billie that he was making a big deal out of all of this. He almost told her this had to be a prank; that it was too farfetched. But he didn't, knowing he would regret that decision later. They rode to the woods next to Mr. Welch's house and threw their bikes down on the ground, landing on the damp leaves. There had been a slight drizzle in this area.

He ran into the woods with Billie by his side. "Over here!"

He headed in the direction of the old beaver pond.

Mick was nervous that Mr. Welch had seen them and wanted to turn around to see if he was coming, but he knew he couldn't stop. There was the crunch of the leaves crackling beneath their feet and the thump of the acorns and pine cones falling to the ground from nearby trees.

Mick saw a squirrel run through the woods and up a tree at the sound of the two kids coming.

Finally, they were there at the beaver pond. Mick smiled. His gaze shifted in the direction of the red Ford Mustang. Only branches and sticks were scattered around on the ground near the water. Mick was puzzled. Bewildered. The Ford was gone.

12

BLACKOUT

"WHERE IS IT?" Billie asked, staring at where she thought it would be.

"It's gone," he whispered.

A hand clamped onto Mick's shoulder. He spun around. His dad was standing there, a gun held tight in his hand.

"Did you finally figure out our secret?" Mick's dad shook his head. "Went here when I told you not to."

"Mr. Welch firing those shots was only an act to make me get scared and stay off his property!" Mick yelled, gritting his teeth.

"Very clever thinking, son," his dad said. His dad stared at him, anger in his eyes.

"I am *not* your son."

Mick dropped to the ground in pain as his dad hit him in the nose with the gun. Billie fell to Mick's side. "MICK!"

Mick's father grabbed Billie, and hit her with a powerful blow to the face. She whimpered, and fell right next to Mick.

Mick clutched his nose, blood dripping down his fingers.

"You kids are so dumb! You thought that we wouldn't catch on to what you were doing?"

Before Mick could pull himself upright, his dad kicked him in the chest, knocking him back down again. Mick grunted and let go of his nose to feel where the shoe had made contact with his chest.

"I feel embarrassed to even be your dad, Mick!"

"Please don't kill us!" Billie screamed, scrambling up from the ground.

Mick's dad took several strides toward her as she screamed and started to run away. He grabbed her hair in one flinching move, pulling it back as she cried out,

"STOP!"

Mick got up this time, forgetting his pain. He bared his teeth.

"LET HER GO!"

His dad pulled Billie in front of him, bringing the gun to her head. She closed her eyes and breathed heavily, tears running down her cheeks.

"What are you going to do about it?" His dad smiled wickedly. "Huh?" He pressed the gun harder against the side of her head.

"LET HER GO! I mean it," Mick cried, taking a step forwards. He clenched his fists and ran towards his dad, letting out a long scream of anguish.

Before he could reach him, Mick was pulled back by two strong hands that threw him to the ground.

Mick winced as Mr. Welch brought down his right foot on Mick's chest, pinning the lad to the ground. He pushed down just forceful enough to prevent him from getting up. Realizing it or not, Mr. Welch was pushing all of the air out of Mick's lungs and he couldn't breathe. Mick grunted from the pain, grabbing Mr. Welch's ankles, wishing he would stop. Mr. Welch pressed his foot harder into the boy's chest, sending several cries from Mick. His face turned a darker shade of red as he struggled to breathe, on the verge of passing out.

His dad pushed Mr. Welch aside. He threw Billie at him and yelled, "Take the girl!"

As Mr. Welch's foot came off of Mick's stomach, he gasped for air like a drowning man breaking the surface of the water. He breathed laboriously, letting the air fill his lungs.

As Mick gasped for breath, a shadow loomed over him. Mick darted his eyes upward. His dad looked down at him, unblinking, his fists balled at his sides.

The last thing Mick heard his dad say, before he brought his foot down on his son's face, making everything go black, was, "Bet you didn't know Mr. Welch was my dad? Did you?"

Billie's scream erupted through the air as she watched Mick's body go limp.

13

SECRETS AND LIES

MICK AWOKE. HIS dad was standing a few feet across from him, Mr. Welch by his side. Billie was sitting there beside him, shaking in fright.

"We're going to die! We're going to die," she mumbled continuously under her breath. Mick couldn't argue with her this time. He was almost certain they would. It was all his fault. Why'd he have to find that deer? If he hadn't of gone back to get it, he never would have gotten caught up in this mystery.

Mick could feel his hands tied behind his back and saw his feet were bound tight with rope.

Mr. Welch took a step towards the two kids. Mick's dad did the same.

"Doesn't my house look nice, Mick?" Mr. Welch asked, almost snarling. "I think it does. It's a shame you have to see it this way!"

"You are never going to get away with this!" Mick yelled.

His dad laughed. Mr. Welch only stared.

"Before we kill you two," began Mick's dad, "we should tell you everything that happened. Since Mr. Welch is my dad, he came up with an idea to rob a bank and put me in charge of doing so. He didn't know I was going to kill the family, but I had no choice. The police were shooting at me and I jumped in a car to escape. The police accidentally killed the woman in the passenger seat when they had been trying to shoot me. I ordered the family to drive me to Mr. Welch's house and they did. Since they knew who I was and where I was headed, I ordered them out of the Ford Mustang with my gun and killed them. I buried them and sunk their car in the old beaver pond to hide the evidence. Meanwhile, one of the family members ended up on the doorstep of a fire department. That was you, Mick."

Anger surged inside him. "You're sick! You killed my parents! How could you? I wish I would've killed you! Just like you killed my family!"

His dad smiled, stepped forward and grabbed Mick's face, making him stare into his eyes. Mick spat, straight into his dad's face, making him stumble back and wipe the saliva. He mumbled an explicative.

"How… is…Mr. Welch…your…dad?" Billie said, her voice shaking in between every word.

Mick's dad growled and showed his teeth. "I was stolen as a baby and Mr. Welch adopted me. I hated being his stepson and growing up in his family. I wanted to grow up and get away. So I married and ended up having my very own adoptive-son. And now I am your dad, Mick."

The monster from deep down inside the man howled with laughter. To Mick, his dad didn't seem human for a few seconds.

"I adopted you to control what you learned. I wanted a child and I wanted you, so I could keep what I did to your family a secret. I am a good man for that,

Mick."

Billie started to have a breakdown. As she cried she shook, almost appearing as if she were convulsing. Her tears flung off her cheeks, falling onto the carpet. She cried so hard it scared Mick.

After several moments, she had almost gotten it back together, crying out, "You didn't want to go to jail! You thought that if you didn't adopt him, that he might figure out that you were the man who killed his parents. If that happened, the police would arrest you. So you did adopt him and controlled everything he learned, careful to make sure he never suspected who he really belonged to!"

Mick stared at this man he had formerly called dad, and wished he could kill him. Wished he was the one with the gun.

"But through the years you made several mistakes! I remember the day you accidentally called me Mick Johnson. Don't you dad?"

His dad's grin was gone, and his face turned a bright red.

"I never thought of that until the other day. I was young and didn't realize that some of my mistakes could cost me everything. That they could reveal my ugly secret I had been working hard not to expose. But look where I am now. The police still haven't caught me or Mr. Welch." Mick's dad's soft, gentle words made Mick boil with fury. "At the time, I was glad that I had changed your name, but I don't see if it would even matter now! The whole town chose to forget about the murders anyway! Why would they want to remember you?"

"What about Mom? What did you do to her?" Mick was ready for the answer. He had to know, even if it killed him.

His dad's smile disappeared, now only replaced with an icy stare. Mick could tell the sudden question surprised him.

"She got suspicious of my past. All those fights that broke out ruined our marriage. I didn't want her to figure out what I had done to your family!"

"Tell me what you did to her!"

His dad gave him a glare that seemed to say 'If I don't, what are you going to do about it?' But after several seconds he began.

"While you were in school, I cooked a big lunch and invited her to eat with me. She never liked to take off work, but I convinced her she needed to. I told her that I wanted to apologize for everything I'd done and told her it would be just me and her. No one there to disturb us." He paused. His lips quivered. "I loved her, Mick, you have to realize that!"

Mick didn't respond. He stared at his dad, trying to read his true emotion.

His dad looked down at the ground, avoiding Mick's stare.

He loved her…isn't that what he said?

Love.

The only thing he loved was seeing her die.

"Before she got home, I set the table and slipped something into her drink. When she got home, she acted so nice. I apologized and everything was fine. Trust me, I started to regret wanting to kill her. I regretted putting that poison into her drink!" He stopped and looked up from the floor, meeting Mick's stare.

Mick saw remorse and regret. But not for a second was he going to forgive him.

"We both sat down. I sat across from her so I could see her fall. So I could see her die." His voice faded and he buried his head in his hands. Mick saw his hands shake and heard his dad's tearful words. "She took a sip and for a second everything was fine. Then, she clutched her throat, fell to the floor, and began foaming at the mouth. I didn't mean…I didn't want…I didn't know," His dad searched for the words until he blurted out, "I needed the insurance money!"

Mick, swelling with rage, yelled, "No you didn't! That's just an excuse!"

"You don't know that!" His dad shook his head.

"Don't act like you don't know what I'm talking about! I remember that day she came in with tears rolling down her face! I remember the nights I hid in my room and listened to the yelling and screaming! I know—"

"Just shut up!" His dad's face turned as red as blood. He reached for his gun.

"You loved her until she got suspicious of your past! Until she had moments when she thought you were hiding things. I know because she told me! When she died, I tried to block my mind of those days when she told me things about you! When she wanted to take me and go live somewhere else! I know this for a fact!"

"You were just a child! You were six! How can you remember?!"

"I REMEMBER *EVERYTHING* ABOUT HER," Mick screamed at the top of his lungs.

Billie shook, and wished she could hide. She wanted to tell Mick to stop. His screaming was only making things worse.

"I remember everything about her!" Mick repeated. "I always will! But *you*! I'll try to forget everything I've ever known about you!"

"JUST SHUT UP! YOU HEAR ME?!" Mick's dad swung forward, putting the gun to Mick's head.

His dad's face was contorted in rage; Mick's a ghostly white. He could feel the gun pressing harder into his skin.

"Stop! Just stop!" Mr. Welch swung his hands outward towards Mick's dad. "We're not here to talk about your wife, Robert! We're here to finish what we started!"

For several seconds Robert Smith held the gun to his son's head. Then, he slowly took it away.

Mick's dad held the gun by his side and looked at Mick.

"You don't want me to shoot you, Mick?"

Mick shook his head, shaking in fear. With his dad's sudden act with the gun, Mick was struck with terror. He gasped for air and took rasping breaths.

Robert Smith aimed the gun at Billie.

"You've made your decision. Now I'll make mine!"

He tightened his grip on the gun and started to pull the trigger.

Mr. Welch jumped.

"Don't! I want to kill them! You had the pleasure of

killing the family and I didn't. Let me kill them!"

"Only Billie! I get to do my son!" Mick's dad exclaimed. Mick had never seen anything like it. They were arguing over which child they got to kill.

Robert Smith grudgingly gave the gun to his father, looking as if he was pouting.

"There's something you didn't tell your son, Robert," Mr. Welch said to Mick's dad while he stared at Billie.

"What?" Mr. Welch's stepson questioned. "Don't just stand there and gossip! Shoot her already!"

"You didn't tell him—"

"WHO CARES WHAT I DIDN'T TELL HIM?! SHOOT THE GIRL!"

Mr. Welch smiled then, a smile that resembled a crazy man. Mr. Welch looked at Mick, staring at him in a sick way. His lips were pulled back into that manic grin, revealing dark yellow teeth. He looked comical, like a grinning animal. To Mick, he looked inhuman.

Mr. Welch averted his stare and grin to Mick's dad. He took a step forward, still aiming the gun at Billie.

"You didn't tell him that I was the one who rescued

him and put him on the fire department steps, did you Robert?"

Mr. Welch took the gun off Billie. Instead, still wearing that same insane smile, he pointed the gun at his stepson.

14
911

ROBERT SMITH, STILL full of rage, didn't even back away. He just stared at the gun his dad was pointing at him.

"I tried to rescue them all but I only got to the baby! I am glad I saved one child. It was my fault that you ended up killing the family. If I hadn't of wanted you to rob the bank, none of this would've happened!" Mr. Welch's deranged smile was gone, replaced with a reddened face and eyes full of loathing for his stepson.

"SHOOT HER, YOU IDIOT! NOT ME!" Robert Smith's face was as red as fire.

"You know why we can't kill Mick! It's one of the main reasons we adopted him!"

"We can't just let them go! They'll tell everyone what we just told them! They'll give us away," Robert Smith declared, moving towards Mr. Welch. "If you're not going to do it, then give the gun to me!"

"Robert, you know why we can't kill him. You know *full* well," Mr. Welch muttered.

Robert Smith stopped and looked down at the floor. Mr. Welch's last words had seemed to knock some sense into him.

Mr. Welch whispered, "Why did you go berserk out there and hit him? You know we are not supposed to interfere until Mick turns twelve!"

Robert Smith's eyes bugged out with malice. "Give me the gun, Dad! GIVE ME THE GUN!"

"You want to know the truth?" Mr. Welch looked deadly serious. Mick's dad tried to back away as Mr. Welch put his finger on the trigger.

"Look, we can work this out. It doesn't have to end this way."

Mr. Welch stared at him like a hawk watching its next meal. "I should've killed you a long time ago."

Mr. Welch pulled the trigger as Billie screamed. The blood from his dad covered Mick's face, making it look like a bad case of the chicken pox.

Mr. Welch's stepson groaned in pain. Blood spurted from his wound, pouring down his hand to his clothes.

Mick couldn't believe what just happened. Mr. Welch had just saved them, Mick once again. His heart was beating out of his chest; his mind in shock. The man who had taken him hunting and taught him how to shoot a rifle, the only guardian who he could remember raising him, was laying there, minutes from death.

"I had to save you two. I know I might be going to jail for conspiracy even though I didn't mean for the murder to happen."

Mr. Welch put the gun at Mick's feet and untied them. Mick rubbed his hands, sore from the loss of circulation. He used his hand to wipe the blood off of his face, spitting some that had gotten into his mouth on the floor, the blood leaving a metallic aftertaste on his tongue. His mind was still in shock. He didn't dare look down at his dad's body.

"Why is the Ford gone?" Mick asked a few moments later, when he was able to speak without losing it.

"We hid it so you didn't have proof for the police."

Mick nodded and looked over at Billie. She was a hundred different emotions all at once. Billie twitched, jerked, and shook, revolted at the scene in front of her. Where one minute she was staring at the body, the next she would have her head turned away, refusing to look. Shock was setting in.

Mick thought he heard her laugh, maybe because of the extreme joy she felt over being saved. The next sound was a whimper like a puppy, and Mick thought she would start crying frenziedly.

Billie still refused to look at the dying man.

Mick's gaze went back and forth to his dad, Billie, and back to Mr. Welch. Mick was overwhelmed by all of this.

"You saved us! You aren't the bad one, you're the good one!" Billie paused. "But why did you do all this?"

Mr. Welch sighed. "Another conversation for another time."

"Did you know it was us the day we went hunting?"

"No, not at all. I didn't know until your dad told me. He didn't care if I knew it was him or not. He knew that I would fire shots like I always do when I see someone on my property. He thought that by me running you off my land, it would scare you enough not to come back and possibly find the car. It was like a miracle to him when the deer he shot went on my property. It was an excuse for him to trespass and for me to shoot at you."

Mick nodded. It was crazy at how calm he was acting. Did he even care that his stepson lay bleeding out on his floor, seconds from death?

Out of the corner of Mick's eye he saw the telephone. He bolted to it, as Mr. Welch screamed at him to stop.

Just as his finger hit the 9, Mr. Welch jerked him backwards. He held a firm grip on the boy's arm.

"Don't call them! I'm not going to jail!"

"And if I don't, who am I to live with? You? People

would get mighty suspicious if I was living with you! You're not even my dad!" Mick stared straight into his eyes, his face inches from Mr. Welch.

After several seconds of intense staring, Mr. Welch let go of his arm and turned around to face Billie.

Mick, pressing the 1 both times, dialed the number and talked to the operator.

"911. What's your emergency?"

"Someone has been shot in Richard Welch's home!" Mick took the phone away from his ear and heard the operator's muffled voice. He hung up.

"Why'd you do that?" Billie asked.

"They know how to get here. Trust me, they've been here before."

Mick rushed towards Robert Smith's body, but Mr. Welch blocked him.

"No! Don't!"

Billie ran towards Mr. Welch, begging, "Please, let me get a cloth! We can stop the blood!"

"NO!" His voice seemed to shatter the air. Mr. Welch grabbed Billie by the arm and bent down in her face. "He deserves to die."

He let go of Billie and put his hands on his hips, letting a long breath escape from his mouth. "I was telling you a lie. I didn't adopt your dad, I stole your dad Mick, when he was just a babe. He was too young to know that he had other parents. I never told him I stole him. He thought I was his real father. I watched someone kill a family but I couldn't let him kill the baby. So I stole him, just like I took you before your dad killed you. History is repeating itself."

The air filled with the sound of sirens as far as back to town. There were numerous vehicles coming, maybe as many as ten, followed by a small fire truck. Among them, an ambulance led the way with a law enforcement SUV on his bumper. The black SUV steered around the ambulance, making sure it got there first.

Mick took a glimpse at Mr. Welch. He had a look of surprise on his face. Mr. Welch ran to the door to let them in. An officer pushed past Mr. Welch, with a hand on the grip of his pistol that was still holstered. Another large, burly policeman with several stripes on his uniform sleeve, probably one of the bosses, asked Mr. Welch to move into the yard while the house filled with police officers and deputy sheriffs.

The first officer that entered looked around the house, room to room, with his gun drawn, spying the two kids, and then speaking into a radio on his shirt. "All clear! Two children and a male victim."

Five officers, one of whom was a woman police investigator with blond hair, took Billie's hand and led her to the kitchen, separating her from Mick. Mick's officer was a younger dark man in a pale blue uniform. He stooped down and looked Mick in the face and calmly asked, "Are you hurt? Are you okay?"

Mick quickly replied, "We're fine. *He* didn't hurt us."

"Who didn't hurt you, the man on the floor or the man in the front yard?" asked the policeman.

"The man in the front yard didn't hurt us. He is Mr. Welch. The man on the floor," Mick pointed at his dad on the floor, "he punched us in the face and tried to kill us!"

15

ASKING QUESTIONS

AFTER HIS DAD was raced to the hospital, the cop who had managed to check if Mick was hurt put him in his police car and took him to the police station.

Billie was placed in an unmarked black SUV by a friendly investigator from the house, who told Billie that she could call her 'Miss Ginger'. The attractive, slim blonde looked like a school teacher instead of a veteran cop. Her faint makeup, hair pulled back in a ponytail like some girls from school, and blue jeans, softened her appearance compared to the uniformed policemen.

Mick was led into the deep and hidden chambers in the back of the large police station. He caught a brief glimpse of Billie and her handler, the blond lady, as they were separated into different rooms. Unknown to both children, Mr. Welch was just a few feet away in a viewing room, surrounded now by five investigators.

Mr. Welch was in Interview Room Five with a red door. Billie was in one of the investigator's office, probably Miss Ginger's, and Mick was in a small room with a green door they called Room One.

For the next hour, the three interviews were conducted. Mr. Welch was gaining the most attention at this point.

In Interview Room Five, a mean looking man with a scar above his right eye sat across from Mr. Welch. He introduced himself as Captain Tillman, but failed to say anything friendly. Another man was standing in the far right corner of the room. His name was James Brown.

"Tell us who the kids are," Captain Tillman said, beginning the interrogation. He leaned back in chair and eyed the old man suspiciously.

"One belongs to my neighbor, the girl was just with him. I don't know her."

"You told my officers you had to shoot your

neighbor, Robert Smith. Is that correct?"

Mr. Welch opened his mouth to speak, but was interrupted by the man standing in the corner. "Captain, Robert Smith is actually his son."

No sign of emotion appeared on the captain's face. It was set in an unemotional frame, giving no clue to how he felt.

"So, he's your son?"

Mr. Welch looked at Captain Tillman with disgust and muttered a weak 'yes'.

The captain shifted in his chair. It was obvious the old man was hiding something. Was this what he hadn't wanted police to find out?

"He was going to kill the kids! I had to save them," Mr. Welch said, avoiding the captain's stare.

"Robert Smith was going to kill his own kid?" Captain Tillman's face twisted in confusion, no longer hiding his emotions.

"Am I going to be charged with something here?" Mr. Welch asked, as if he were losing interest.

Captain Tillman's face darkened. "Answer the

question."

"If you're going to arrest me, you better do it."

"Answer the question!" The captain yelled, slamming his fist down on the table. "It's that simple!"

Mr. Welch gave a sly smile to Captain Tillman, knowing with his next words the interrogation would end. Mr. Welch took a short intake of breath and then said, raising his head in confidence, "I'm done! I want my lawyer."

. . . .

Investigator Jones, a dark young man, with the build of a football player, smiled at Mick in Interview Room One, offering him some water. "My friends call me Gator. I used to play for the Florida Gators, but I was too small for the NFL."

"I'm Mick Smith," replied Mick, refusing to smile, still shook up from what had happened just thirty minutes ago. "I mean," Mick replied, shaking his head in realization, "I'm Mick Johnson."

Gator stared at Mick for a moment, looking at the shaken young boy. He wondered what was going through the child's mind. All Gator knew was that Richard Welch—someone he strongly disliked based on past dealings with the man—had saved the children from being killed and that another man was dead. He looked down at his notes, wondering who this boy really was. Gator had his own suspicions at what had really taken place in that house but he knew he had to stay on script. It was time to get started.

"Tell me what happened."

"My dad, the man on the floor, was going to kill me and Billie," Mick blurted.

"Let's slow down and you tell me how you ended up in Mr. Welch's house."

Mick shuffled his feet. "Well, we lived next door and had suspected Mr. Welch of some bad stuff."

For the next two hours, Mick told him everything. Ten minutes into the story, the cop with the scar joined Gator and sat in a chair and listened.

. . . .

In Ginger's office, Billie sat in a chair across from Ginger. Ginger was nice and helped Billie stay relaxed and calm.

"My name is Ginger," she told Billie again. "I am going to ask you a few questions and you answer as best as you can, okay? We've called your dad and he is coming."

Billie nodded.

"Tell me what happened."

"I went with Mick to Mr. Welch's house to look at something and we were bound and gagged by Mick's father, Robert Smith. I was so scared! I thought we were going to die."

"What were you going to look at?"

"The red Ford Mustang in Mr. Welch's old beaver pond. Mick found it when his dad shot a deer. He said it had appeared to have been sunk in the pond."

"Is that all that happened? Why was Robert Smith shot?"

The cop's words made the image of Robert Smith's body falling to the floor replay itself in the young girl's mind. She knew that that image would never truly go away. She could see it every time she closed her eyes.

"Robert Smith was going to kill us and Mr. Welch saved us by shooting him."

"Why was he going to shoot you?"

At that point, Billie told her everything she needed to know. She started when Mick first talked to her about it, to them researching the car, going to the library and them almost being killed by Mick's dad, Robert Smith.

. . . .

Ginger, Gator, and Captain Tillman sat around a table with a man in a suit from the State Attorney's office, the county sheriff, (whose name was Bill Dailey) and two other officers. For forty minutes they compared the stories of Mick and Billie.

"Sergeant Miles took Gandy to the pond. No car, but there were signs something was pulled out and moved within the last few days. They are posting a BOLO up and down the highway," stated Captain Tillman.

"Junk yards are our best bet," said Sheriff Dailey.

"So, you believe these kids?" asked the lawyer from the State Attorney's Office.

149

Heads nodded in agreement around the table. One question came from the oldest veteran of the group.

"Can we get Drake out-of-retirement to help us with the missing person's case from the archives? Robert Smith may not be Robert Smith, just like this Johnson boy may have family still alive."

16

CHASING CLUES

GINGER GOT OUT of her car and approached the old bearded man in the junkyard. Mr. Darby had owned the junkyard for years, cars as far as the eye could see. She flirted with the old man by paying him a compliment.

"If I didn't know better, I'd say you must have landed that new girlfriend. You look great!"

The old bearded man grinned with snuff-stained teeth and asked, "You didn't look me up to ask me out?"

Ginger felt herself blush, realizing the old man was flirting too.

"No, just business. Looking for some cars."

"I told those other cops all I know," the junkyard owner said. He seemed genuine. Ginger suspected he was very clever.

"I know you aren't interested in the large reward, but if you aren't involved, you don't have anything to worry about. I know how you feel about sticking your nose in other people's business," said Ginger, picking her words carefully.

"I don't tell on people. I mind my own business, but I do see things."

"You are like a large owl; you see everything!" replied Ginger, stroking the man's pride.

"Might know a man who was paid to crush an old Mustang….he took the money but sold it to a dealer in Florida. '64 Ford Mustang could bring a fortune."

"No, something a little newer. 2001, red Ford Mustang."

"Refused one that had been in a flood. Joker brought one by and wanted it crushed, but I sent him over to Jakes' Metal Company. Does that help any?" The old man smiled and waited for a look of pleasure from the young cop.

"Why, Mr. Darby, that may be the winning prize.

Reward?"

"Yeah, sign me up if it pans out."

. . . .

Ginger called Captain Tillman and told him the news. She waited for Gator, Captain Tillman, several uniformed officers, and Sheriff Dailey who arrived in three separate SUV's. They entered Jakes' Metal Company by driving through the main gate and parked among hundreds of crushed vehicles, which were waiting to be loaded on large trucks.

Gator sprinted to the back of the yard where a forklift was running. Sheriff Dailey went to the office, accompanied by two uniformed deputies, and Ginger and Captain Tillman moved up another row of cars. The junked vehicles were stacked ten high in the crushed pile. Green, silver, and black automobiles waiting to be crushed were stacked three high.

Ginger pulled her black pistol and moved up a row of cars opposite Captain Tillman. Her radio barked a command from him.

"Look for the crusher! It will be toward the back!"

Just as Captain Tillman finished speaking, another voice spoke from the radio.

"Gator found a blue tarp covering a vehicle. It's drained green and brown rusty water on the dirt. Looks like it came from a swamp."

Gator peeked under the tarp and reached for his radio.

"Captain, found one under a tarp. Send Paul to keep this area secure while I move up to the fork lift."

"Stay there! We are moving in on the fork lift driver."

Ginger found the crusher, a massive hydraulic monster used to flatten automobiles into six foot cubes of metal. A man was pouring red fluid from a bright yellow, five gallon plastic jug into a reservoir on the crusher. Black hoses and a controller led away from the machine where an operator would stand and control the machine. With a car loaded by a forklift into the holder, hydraulic jaws would push down and up, crushing the car into a condensed mass that looked like a metal cube.

Captain Tillman and Ginger approached the worker, both holding their pistols out-stretched toward the man's back.

"Stand up and keep your hands in the air where we can see them!" ordered Captain Tillman.

The man dropped the jug, the red liquid spilling onto the ground. He held up his grease stained hands and slowly turned and faced the cops.

"State your name!"

"Jake Martin! I'm the owner."

Captain Tillman put Jake Martin into his police car and took him back to the police station to question him. After an hour interrogation, Jake was released. No charges were filed against him. He told Captain Tillman that Robert Smith had wanted the car crushed and gave him one hundred dollars the day before.

17

NEVER SAY GOODBYE

MICK AND BILLIE were heroes in town now. Kids around school would even walk up and congratulate them. Word had spread that they were the two who had found the red Ford mustang in Welch's old beaver pond. A newspaper article came out about the car. The article read:

Red Ford Mustang Found

The Johnson family remains missing

Two kids found a red Ford Mustang in Richard Welch's old beaver pond, believed to belong to the Johnson's who disappeared eleven years ago. Police have not found the missing family but have been told

that one of the two kids was the child found on the fire department steps when the family disappeared. Richard Welch was charged with several counts of conspiracy and involvement in a bank robbery. Police are trying to determine his link to the missing family. He will be going on trial at the end of the summer. Police suspect that Robert Smith was the man who robbed the Henry County Bank and used the Ford Mustang to escape the police eleven years ago. Robert Smith suffered a gunshot wound and was found dead in Richard Welch's home. The police have determined a possible motive for Robert Smith's death. They think that Richard Welch and Robert Smith were accomplices in the bank robbery and the disappearance of the Johnson family who have been missing since 2003. They also believe Richard Welch was responsible in Robert Smith's death. Police have failed to have any leads into the Johnson family's disappearance until this recent event. The two kids will be recognized on the Henry County News. The relatives of the child from the missing family still

haven't been identified and the child will remain in a foster home. This story was submitted by David Brewer of the Summersville Daily News.

For now, Mick was staying with a foster family even though Billie had hoped Mick could live with her. Her dad had told her that he probably would be living with some of his family after the police identified them.

Soon, the two kids were recognized on the Henry County News for finding the red Ford Mustang. Billie, who was smiling ear to ear after their appearance on TV, walked around with Mick in the parking lot as they talked.

"Even if the police never solve the case, we both will know the truth," Mick said.

Billie leaned forward and whispered in his ear, "Even Mr. Welch will know. But somehow the truth always reveals itself. Give it time, Mick, soon everyone will know."

Mick, debating on whether to say it or not, made up his mind and mumbled, "We can't trust him."

"No, we can't," Billie said. "Even though he saved us."

She took a deep breath and exhaled loudly.

"Billie, he put me on the fire department steps for a reason. I have a feeling he didn't just do it to save a child from being killed."

Billie nodded. "There's a reason behind it, alright. Some part of me makes me think it's definitely not a good one."

Billie and Mick looked at each other for several seconds in complete silence. Mick was about to speak when Billie caught him off guard. He didn't know what had just hit him, but for a tenth of a second he had seen Billie in a different way. He gazed into her eyes and at her face, wanting to look into her soul. She looked so alluring, so…beautiful.

Mick, afraid Billie would notice him staring, looked away.

"I'm sorry about your mother," Billie said.

Mick was the one who nodded this time. He took a deep breath inside, thankful she hadn't noticed him.

"I shouldn't have been feeling sorry for myself, but for you instead. The only father you ever knew did kill your mother. I just hope that is not what happened with my mother."

"It's okay." Mick didn't want to think about his mom at the moment. If he did, he might just break down in tears.

Mick, wanting to cry, wished everything was back to normal. He wished his real family had never been killed. Even though he knew his foster family was waiting on him, he turned to Billie.

"Goodbye," Mick said, saying the word he wished he would never have to say.

He would only see her at school now. His new set of parents banned him from seeing her, thinking she would only make him relive those terrible times in his past. In their mind, she was more of a reminder of all he'd been through than anything else. He even heard a rumor that his foster family might be moving to a different town.

Billie, whose dad was waiting anxiously for her to hurry up, smiled and said, "Never say good-bye."

She wrapped her arms around him in an embrace before Mick could stop her.

Mick let out a yelp, surprised at her boldness. His heart raced and he felt the blood flood his face. He put both hands around her shoulder, until he was brave enough to hug her like he should. His hands moved to her back, and he hugged her tight, enjoying the closeness.

This was the first hug Mick had had in a long while and he didn't want her to ever let go. He put his head on her shoulder, and let the tears finally break through. They soaked her shirt, and he began to shake uncontrollably.

"I know how you feel," Billie said, seeming to read his thoughts. "I know how it feels to lose the one person who understood you."

Mick had lost everything: his family, the only mom and dad he knew, and the life that had just been swept away from him. He had no one he could count on, no one he could trust. No one who loved him.

Mick hugged Billie even harder. Except for *her*.

Finally, they let go of each other. Billie smiled at Mick and they wiped the tears from their eyes.

"See ya cowgirl!"

"Wow!" Billie smiled. "You finally got something right."

Mick laughed.

And then they walked away from each other, without looking back. They wouldn't see each other as much as they had become accustomed to, yet Mick remained hopeful that he would see her a lot more than he thought he would.

Neither of them realized this was only the beginning. Mick and Billie were just kids; they didn't know what dangers were in store for them. If only the two knew what truths would be brought to the light and what secrets Summersville had to hide.

There are secrets in every town, but in Summersville, secrets are everywhere.

. . . .

Billie stared out the window. Silence filled the car. Creepy, eerie silence.

"You know, Dad, I thought I would figure out what happened to Mom through all of this. I don't know why I thought that, but I did. And yet, I never figured out anything."

Her dad laid his hand on top of hers and sighed.

I shouldn't have brought this up, Billie thought.

For nights and nights after her mom's disappearance, her dad had held her and they would just cry. At the time, it was the only thing they could do. Now, Billie had to help her mom. She just had to find out what had happened to her.

"You know that we shouldn't worry about your mother. Sooner or later we'll know the truth. Let's just focus on our lives right now."

Billie knew the conversation was over, but she had to ask a question. A question that she knew would send her dad into a fit, but possibly wasn't afraid to answer.

"Dad, did you kill Mom?"

The brakes squealed on the asphalt as the car came to a screeching halt. Her dad looked her dead in the eye.

"Never ask me that again! You hear me!?"

....

The librarian popped three quarters into the newspaper machine. As she pulled one out, the front cover caught her eye. She just about fainted as she read the headline: *Red Ford Mustang Found.*

She couldn't believe it! Was this true? She read the article and turned around to find Mick.

"Dear me!" she shouted, holding a hand to her heart. "You scared me!"

Maybe this was a bad idea, Mick thought.

"You know, I should have never doubted you and your friend. The two of you… aren't exactly ordinary."

Mick smiled a sleepy grin. "I just wanted to thank you and tell you that you were wrong about us."

"Thank me? Why?"

"Because when you told me and my friend that we could never solve the case, it gave me determination. I wanted to solve the case even more just to show you. That's why I'm thanking you."

The librarian said, "Well, if you need some more of that determination, just call me and I'll try to help…by being negative."

The old woman laughed.

Mick was exhausted. Completely drained. He didn't really want to talk to her but knew he should. As he started to leave, the librarian shouted, "Wait! I have a question."

Mick stopped dead in his tracks. "I'll have an answer."

"What are you going to name the case, dear? You have to have a name."

Mick bit his lip and tried to think. Then before he could change his mind, exclaimed, "The Forgotten Headline!"

"I love it! You know me and Mr. Welch used to be married?"

Mick gasped. "No way!"

"Yes. Back then he was a good man. He had his problems but we all do. Now I realize he's not the man he used to be..."

"No, I'm pretty sure that's not the case anymore."

The librarian nodded. "Well, I'll see you around,

Mick. Who knows what other things you'll find out in this town."

He told her bye and climbed back into the car with his new family.

18

THE TRIAL

INSIDE, MR. WELCH was secretly smiling. The jury had fallen for all the tricks and lies that the lawyer had presented. Mr. Welch couldn't believe what he was seeing. He might just get away with this in spite of some very bad luck on his part. One theory was that he shot Robert Smith in self-defense. Another was that Robert Smith acted alone and the jury doubted the prosecution's evidence.

Billie, whether she was afraid or just nervous, had been a lousy witness. In her testimony, she failed to cry when she needed to cry and failed to look pitiful when she needed to look pitiful. In so many words, the prosecutor had not coached her well enough.

"You're confusing me...it's not fair...I didn't mean that. You're putting words in my mouth," said Billie while being grilled by Mr. Welch's attorney.

"He told us that he stole Mick's adoptive father! He also said that he was the one who came up with the idea to rob the bank! If he hadn't of wanted his stepson to do this, Mick's family wouldn't be dead," she said.

"Your Honor, I request that her testimony be stricken from the record because it is hearsay and it can't be substantiated," said the defense attorney to the judge.

"That's not fair," cried Billie. "You're not listening to me! All he is doing is trying to make it look like I don't know what I'm talking about!"

The judge rapped his gavel on the bench and firmly said to Billie, "Young lady, you will keep your comments to the question that was asked! Her last statement will be removed from the record!"

The court reporter obeyed.

The prosecutor stood up with rage and yelled, "I object!"

"Overruled," said the judge. With that, the

prosecutor sat back down in defeat.

Mr. Welch was seen smiling. This made Billie even more furious, not wanting Mr. Welch to win.

The defense called Mick to the stand next. Everyone in the courtroom had a bad feeling about Mick's emotional state.

"Weren't you just mad at your dad and Mr. Welch because your life turned out so miserable?" the defense attorney asked Mick. Mick didn't even get a chance to answer the first question before he asked him the second.

"Isn't it true that you wanted to kill your dad, yourself, and Mr. Welch? How did you feel when your dad hit you? Did you really shoot your dad and blame Mr. Welch?"

The prosecutor stood and yelled again, "I object to this questioning!"

Mick tried to answer the second or third question, but became completely confused when he heard what had come out of the defense attorney's mouth.

"I didn't shoot anybody…this isn't fair…it's all a

bunch of lies," cried Mick as he stood in anger.

"No more questions!" said the defense attorney as he sat down, further irritating Mick who was completely frustrated.

Mick stood and yelled at the judge, "Do something!" At this point, Mick's face was twisted as if he were in pain, tears falling down his cheeks. He had completely lost it. Through all the sobs, Mick said, "Mr. Welch came up with a plan to rob a bank…" He was cut off by the judge who pounded his gavel on the bench to gain control of the courtroom.

Hushes, moans, and voices could be heard from the courtroom. The judge continued to pound his gavel, furious that he had managed to lose control. "Order in the court or I will have all of you removed!" Then he turned to Mick and said, "Witness is dismissed!"

Mick's fury and rage had reached a high point. A court bailiff took Mick by the arm and removed him from the witness box.

The judge commanded, "Remove him from the courtroom!"

Meanwhile, Mr. Welch was smiling. He knew he had won.

Later that afternoon, the jury returned with a verdict.

The judge ordered Mr. Welch to stand. "Will the defendant please rise?"

Mr. Welch complied along with the other attorneys.

"Foreman of the jury, do you have a verdict?"

"Yes, your Honor, we do."

. . . .

After ten minutes of being lectured by one of the assistant state attorneys in the hallway, Mick was told to keep his mouth shut and stand against the wall and wait for his next instructions.

Mick protested, "Why can't I be in the courtroom? Why'd you throw me out? I was just trying to tell my story!"

The attorney pointed a finger at Mick and repeated, "Not another word or the judge can have you removed from the whole building!"

With that, the attorney re-entered the courtroom, leaving Mick to stand with some clerk he didn't know. From a distance, it was obvious Mick was pouting and he continued to fume, although he didn't say anything.

Mick turned to the clerk. "None of this is fair! They're going to let Mr. Welch get away with murder!"

The clerk reminded Mick, "He probably saved your life and you don't realize it! Be grateful instead of acting like a spoiled brat!"

Mick's bottom lip poked out farther than the top while he gave the clerk an evil stare. He turned his back on her and sat down on a bench. Mick replayed his last few minutes in the courtroom and sighed. He didn't want to admit it but he had lost his cool and it made him look childish. He couldn't believe the defense attorney wouldn't even let him answer the question. Mick had even rehearsed his lines over and over again so he could look credible in the courtroom. But that didn't matter now. He had blown it.

Mick thought about what he should have said, and when he should have stopped talking to regain his control. He slapped his forehead with his hand. "I can't believe I let this happen! I'm so stupid!"

His thoughts went to Billie and he wondered where they had taken her. Did she have to leave the courtroom, too?

The assistant state attorney stormed out the back door of the courtroom returning to Mick's side. Anger was all over his face. His eyes bugged out. He stammered as he tried to find his words while confronting Mick.

Mick, taking a step back, was afraid of what the man was fixing to do to him.

"Do you know what's going on in there, young man?" the attorney asked.

"No."

"The jury is eating all that bull up and we might not be able to fix it."

Mick sighed. He wanted to kick something. He mumbled to the attorney and said, "I saw Mr. Welch smiling."

The man replied, "He thinks he is winning. We

still have a couple tricks up our sleeve."

As the attorney walked away, Mick whispered, "I wished I would've killed him." He imagined the bullet entering Mr. Welch's head as he pulled an invisible trigger.

. . . .

Billie was in the bathroom. She had finally stopped crying. Her emotions had turned from humiliation to hate. She felt herself getting mad but her thoughts were running clearer instead of all jumbled up like they had been on the witness stand.

Her thoughts finally turned to Mick. Even though she had done poorly herself, she felt terrible for him. She wished it had been her who had been thrown out of the courtroom. She kicked the trash can and her thoughts were interrupted by a voice at the bathroom door.

"Billie, are you okay?"

Billie stopped abruptly and picked up the trash can, turning it upright.

"I'm coming, Dad!"

Didn't he understand that she wasn't okay? Did he

realize what she was going through? Besides, she was only eleven years old, what did he expect? Her sassy attitude had returned. She started to feel normal again.

She opened the bathroom door and met her dad who said to her, "I was starting to worry about you! You've been in there twenty minutes!"

Billie ignored him and said, "Dad, why did that man try to put words in my mouth?! He made me so confused!"

Her dad started the explanation by saying, "Billie, we didn't prepare you well enough for that. Even adults have problems being questioned by professionals who do this for a living. It's not fair but…" Her dad was cut off by Billie's insistent questioning.

"Why are they going to let Mr. Welch get away with this?"

Her dad reached forward to hug her, and she fell into his arms. She could feel the tears starting to form again.

"Honey, this is just how the court system works. Besides, anything could happen," Billie's dad said, a smile forming on his lips. "It's not over yet."

For the next few minutes, Billie cried into her dad's shirt, while he rubbed her back and said, "Don't worry. We're not going to let Mr. Welch get away with this."

....

Mr. Welch stood. Everything seemed to slow down. He replayed all that had happened back in his mind. He could see Mick crying and the bailiff taking his arm; he could see Billie getting frustrated; he could see the prosecutor's stupid objections which the judge ignored. His final thought before the verdict was read was, *I'm going to get away with this.*

Mr. Welch couldn't help but smile. He knew what the verdict was going to be.

"We the Jury find Richard Welch..." There was a short pause.

"Not guilty on all counts."

EPILOGUE

MR. WELCH FILLED his glass with wine. He let the liquid run down his throat and he raised the glass in triumph.

Now that he was back home and free, a thought occurred to him. It was as if something was revealed to him. The thought was that he should kill the kids the first opportunity offered to him.

His next immediate thought was that he should have killed the two kids after he killed Robert Smith, and blamed it on Smith.

He cursed as he slammed his fist down on the countertop.

Through his anger, his mind went back to the trial. He wished he could have videotaped Mick and Billie. The jurors were probably laughing along with him now. Who believed kids anyway?

Mr. Wells decided he couldn't kill Mick just yet. He would have to wait. Mr. Welch still remembered the reason he kept Mick alive. Heck, he had killed his own son to keep Mick from being killed just for that specific reason. Mick should be grateful to Mr. Welch. He had saved his life. Mick's family owed him. Soon, he would get what he wanted and then he would kill Mick after he was done with him.

Mr. Welch plopped down in his recliner, let out a long sigh, closed his eyes and let the thoughts run through his mind. He thought about the day he had put Mick on the fire department steps. He remembered the gunshots and screams. He also remembered when he snatched the baby from the car.

There was a reason why he put Mick on the fire department steps. There was a reason why he didn't let his stepson kill Mick and there was a reason why he had to keep Mick alive, even if it meant protecting him. No, he didn't mean for his stepson to kill that family but he realized it happened all for the better.

Mr. Welch smiled, his depression replaced with a

goal that steered him away from being suicidal.

Mr. Welch knew he was bad. He knew that he had had plenty of chances to do the right thing to avoid being a bad person. But he hadn't accepted those chances.

Mr. Welch had killed his own stepson. Was it because of pure selfishness? Did he only kill him so he wouldn't hurt Mick? Was it just pure greed?

Mr. Welch was not a good person. His actions to save the kids from being killed didn't make him a hero; he had done it for a selfish reason. Mr. Welch had to be bad, and there seemed to be no other way for him to live.

The reason that he had gotten away with it all seemed to shock him. He had fooled everyone. He guessed everyone saw him as a man that had defeated the bad guy and prevented two kids from being killed. They didn't realize how much he had played them.

A small tap on the door startled Mr. Welch. He didn't usually get company. He stuck his free hand in his pocket and found his way to the door.

He grasped the doorknob, and then flung it open. All Mr. Welch saw before he fell to the floor at the front door, screaming and cursing, was a gun.

The flash of the explosion almost blinded him. He grasped his shoulder, and felt where he had been shot.

"That's for what you and Robert Smith did to me all these years," the feminine voice said. "You couldn't keep me locked up forever, Richard."

Mr. Welch got a glimpse of the girl before she ran down the porch steps, realizing just who she was.

"I'll find my brother," the woman screamed, her shrill, high voice finding its way into Mr. Welch's ears.

He watched her run off into the night, as the darkness seemed to swallow her up.

Do you have questions?

What was the reason Mr. Welch kept Mick alive?

Why did Mr. Welch keep Mick's sister locked up?

Will she find Mick before Mr. Welch finds her?

What happened to Billie's mother?

To get the answers

Read Book 2 of the Summersville series

SECRET TRUST

Available soon

ACKNOWLEDGEMENTS

THE BOOK that you are holding in your hands (or reading through your device) took over two years to complete, and without the help from my beta readers and other supporters, it would not have been possible.

It was my desire to create a darker, grittier mystery for older kids who haven't yet developed a love for reading. I believe too many mysteries for the upper elementary and middle grade range try to hide the dark truths and make everything seem to work out in the end.

I want to give a shout out to my amazing beta readers, who dedicated their time and effort to read my drafts and helped to perfect my work: Hope Allen, Olivia Garret, Jessica Daniel, Tammy Cosson, Rodney Free, Pam Beck, Dan Owens, Hannah Dawkins, Cathy Hall, Chasity Kemp, Noel Dahl, and also to my parents. You guys are the best! Special thanks to the teachers and staff at West DeFuniak Elementary School who encouraged my love for reading and writing.   Much appreciation to my fellow peers for reading my work and listening tirelessly to me talk about it. Gratitude for Mr. Dan Owens, Director of the DeFuniak Springs Library, who connected me to other authors which began my journey to publish this book. I can't thank you enough for your great help.

Also, I want to thank my editor, Josh Vogt, for all the encouraging comments and honest feedback. Whitney Evans, this book wouldn't look the way it does if it wasn't for you.

To the readers: Thank you so much for picking up my book! If you can, please leave a review on Goodreads, Amazon, or any other fine book retailer. I hope you enjoy this installment of the Summersville series and further mysteries to come.

ABOUT THE AUTHOR

McCaid Paul is 14 years old and lives on a farm in a rural community in Northwest Florida. He enjoys hiking, traveling, and being in nature. He developed a passion for reading at an early age. In first grade, McCaid learned to journal which developed into a love of writing. His inspiration to become an author came from his dad, Joel, who wrote many interesting stories for his son. McCaid is a fan of anything crime or mystery. The Forgotten Headline is his fictional debut.

Check him out on his website
www.mccaidpaulbooks.com
Or on Twitter
@MccaidP

CPSIA information can be obtained
at www.ICGtesting.com
Printed in the USA
LVHW090059170521
687004LV00032B/501/J